"Your father warned me away ___ you, Jess."

Jess froze, eyes fixed on Kate, while people streamed around them. It was one thing for him and his dad to disagree, but he was stunned and disappointed that his father had hurt Kate.

She kicked at a stone on the ground with the tip of her boot. "He told me I wasn't good enough for you and that I should back away."

"Is that why you left?" He asked the question that had haunted him for ten years.

"I was always going to leave. I told you that. You didn't listen. Your father's words… Maybe they helped me to justify walking away."

"He was wrong, Kate." The words burst from Jess's lips as their impact barreled straight into his gut. Could he have prevented Kate from leaving? Did it matter anymore?

She stared at him, eyes round.

"You know that, right?" he persisted.

"I'm not sure what I know, Jess…"

Tina Radcliffe has been dreaming and scribbling for years. Originally from Western New York, she left home for a tour of duty with the US Army Security Agency stationed in Augsburg, Germany, and ended up in Tulsa, Oklahoma. Her past careers include certified oncology RN, library cataloger and pharmacy clerk. She recently moved from Denver, Colorado, to the Phoenix, Arizona, area, where she writes heartwarming and fun inspirational romance.

Books by Tina Radcliffe

Love Inspired

Hearts of Oklahoma

Finding the Road Home
Ready to Trust
His Holiday Prayer
The Cowgirl's Sacrifice

Big Heart Ranch

Claiming Her Cowboy
Falling for the Cowgirl
Christmas with the Cowboy
Her Last Chance Cowboy

The Rancher's Reunion
Oklahoma Reunion
Mending the Doctor's Heart

Visit the Author Profile page
at Harlequin.com for more titles.

The Cowgirl's Sacrifice

Tina Radcliffe

LOVE INSPIRED
INSPIRATIONAL ROMANCE

LOVE INSPIRED®
INSPIRATIONAL ROMANCE

Recycling programs
for this product may
not exist in your area.

ISBN-13: 978-1-335-40941-6

The Cowgirl's Sacrifice

Copyright © 2021 by Tina M. Radcliffe

This edition published by arrangement with Harlequin Books S.A.

For questions and comments about the quality of this book, please contact us
at CustomerService@Harlequin.com.

Love Inspired
22 Adelaide St. West, 40th Floor
Toronto, Ontario M5H 4E3, Canada
www.Harlequin.com

Printed in U.S.A.

Being confident of this very thing,
that he which hath begun a good work in you
will perform it until the day of Jesus Christ.
—*Philippians* 1:6

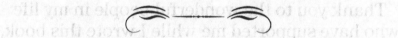

Book four of the Hearts of Oklahoma series owes a bit of gratitude to Lisa at Dr. Judy Huey's office because her hair inspired Kate Rainbolt's rebel hair. I'd also like to give a shout-out to a real Rainbolt, reader Jordan Rainbolt.

Thank you to the wonderful people in my life who have supported me while I wrote this book, with extra hugs going to my Wrangler Team and my morale builders, Steph, Sherri and Rogenna. Thank you to Tom Radcliffe for always listening. You bless me daily. A final thank-you to superagent Jessica Alvarez, who has all the answers.

Chapter One

❧

Kate Rainbolt's gaze followed the man
who entered Eagle Donuts. He moved
past the tables of early morning customers
with smooth, long-limbed confidence. A
tall man, he wore a black barn coat, faded
jeans and scuffed boots, not unlike dozens
of other Oklahoma cowboys.

She was ready to dismiss him when
something set off an internal warning,
urging her to take a second glance. Kate
tensed and stepped away from the counter, feigning interest in a display of coffee
mugs. When the cowboy lifted his head
and tipped back the brim of his hat to as-
sess the inside of the shop, she saw his

face, and her heart slammed against her chest.

Jess McNally.

She'd been back in Rebel for an hour, and naturally, she'd run into her former beau.

Her only beau.

Usually, Kate kept her emotions hidden behind a mask of greasepaint and an outrageous, red felt cowboy hat. But she wasn't a rodeo clown any longer, and it would take work to hide the emotions rocking her to the core. The last time she'd seen Jess was ten years ago, when she'd rejected his marriage proposal.

It was unfortunate that time had only improved his good looks. Dark hair peeked out from beneath a black Stetson, and a scruffy five o'clock shadow emphasized the angles of his face.

Jess's slate-gray eyes connected with hers, and she froze, chin down, her gaze going everywhere but back to the cowboy in front of her. She willed her pulse to slow before she dared to meet his gaze again.

Ten years. He should not have this effect on her after all that time.

"Kate?"

"Hey, Jess." She shoved her left hand in her coat pocket, ignoring the twinge in her casted arm and the pain that shot through her middle as she jostled her tender rib cage.

"You're back in Rebel?" he asked.

She lifted her face. "For now, I am. What about you?"

"Yeah. I've been back for a few weeks."

"So you're visiting?" She prayed that his next words would be that he was leaving town soon. Regret wasn't on her schedule today, and she lacked the mental stamina for a what-if game about whether or not she'd walked away from the best thing that had ever happened to her.

"Visiting? No." He said the words slowly, paused and looked at her.

A shiver galloped down Kate's arms.

"I guess Reece didn't mention..." Jess ran a hand over his face.

"Reece?" Her second eldest big brother

hadn't said anything special when she'd called to let him know she was on her way from Tucson, only that it was about time. His mantra du jour.

"I'm the foreman at Rebel Ranch," Jess said. "New position."

Kate blinked and focused her attention on the tips of her hand-tooled Western boots while trying not to reveal how surprised she was. Because she was absolutely surprised. She'd been offered the position of ranch foreman at Christmas. Her brothers Reece and Mitch ran the popular guest ranch and had mentioned it to Kate at their brother Tucker's wedding.

"Reece is expanding the cattle side. I'll be supervising production and care of livestock and horses."

"Yes. I know about the expansion," she said. Though she worked to keep her voice neutral, anxiety had her gnawing on her lip.

There was another lengthy pause between them. Jess hesitated as if measuring his words. "Is my taking this job a problem?"

There was no way she'd answer a loaded question like that. She was going to be living at the ranch temporarily. Even short-term, that would be way too close to Jess McNally, the man who had somehow managed to steal her job right out from under her. Yes, there would definitely be problems. Several of them.

Kate glanced at the wall clock. "If you'll excuse me. I have to be somewhere." She nodded to Jess. "It seems I'll be seeing you around."

Confusion now shone in his eyes. Well, she didn't blame him. She was confused too.

A stop just outside of town to fill her truck with gas and check the tires proved frustrating. Kate struggled to complete the task with the use of only her right arm, once again realizing how much she'd taken having two functional arms for granted. Okay, so it was awkward, and yes, she was in pain. However, she knew she was blessed to be alive after a one-on-one with a bull, and she was grateful. The accident had caused her to reflect on life and led her back to Oklahoma until she could figure out what she was going to do going forward.

Before hopping back into the truck, Kate made a cursory check of the covered flatbed on the ancient pickup that held all her worldly possessions. All of them, except her horse. She'd left Einstein in Tucson. A friend would drop the gelding off when she passed through Oklahoma in a day or so. Kate had sold her own horse trailer weeks ago to make a dent in medical bills and pay for the room she'd rented while she recuperated.

Twenty minutes later, the trailer hitch jangled as she turned onto the ranch road. The elaborate metalwork double R on the archway over the gate to Rebel Ranch greeted her. The sight of the entrance against the early April blue sky cheered her spirits.

Spring in Oklahoma. That meant the promise of azaleas, tulips, dogwoods and wisteria in the days and weeks to come. Today, the blossoming redbud along the tree-lined drive had already exploded with bright pink-and-purple flowers. She eased off the gas pedal to appreciate their beauty before guiding the truck to the Rebel Ranch main house, where the offices and VIP guest suites were located.

Kate got out, shrugged off her jacket, and glanced around.

Rebel Ranch.

It was twenty-two years ago this month that her momma passed and her daddy took off, leaving the younger Rainbolts to be raised by their big brothers. Yes, those events had triggered huge changes for the five Rainbolt siblings. They'd inherited the undeveloped land that had belonged to their maternal grandfather. Six years ago, Reece had formulated a plan to turn the property into a guest ranch. By then, Kate had already been chasing her rodeo dreams.

It was good to be back, even though Rebel Ranch hadn't always exactly been home. A double-wide on the other side of town had been her real home growing up. They were dirt poor in those days, but they'd had each other.

"Bug?"

Kate whirled around at the nickname and grinned, joy flooding her heart. Mitch, the eldest Rainbolt, stood outside the doors of the two-story house that served as the administrative headquarters.

Mitch. The family rock. He strode across the gravel and was at her side in a heartbeat.

"I've missed you, big brother."

"You too, Bug." Ladybug Rainbolt, he called her, because she was forever flying away.

Mitch pressed a kiss to her forehead and stepped back. "I guess I better not hug you." He eyed her casted arm and frowned. "You didn't mention a broken arm."

"It wasn't worth mentioning."

"Yeah. Wait until Reece finds out. He'll have something to say. Count on it." Mitch looked around. A few curious ranch hands observed them from afar. "Where's your trailer?"

"Sold it."

Her brother frowned. "And your horse?"

"He'll be here in a few days."

"Sounds like you have a story to tell. Let's go inside."

"Can a girl get a cup of coffee?" she asked.

"Yes, ma'am. A fresh pot for Bug Rainbolt. Have you eaten lately?"

Kate grimaced, recalling how she'd almost scored Eagle donuts. She'd been dreaming about those donuts for a good long time. Another black mark on Jess McNally's record. He'd disturbed her peace of mind and her breakfast.

"I could use a little snack," she admitted.

"Eagle donuts work for you? We have your favorite."

"Apple fritters?" She sighed with anticipation. "Oh, yeah. Now you're talking my love language."

"I wish I had your metabolism," Mitch

said. "You have no idea the havoc my wife's pies are playing on me."

Kate chuckled in response. As they headed to the ranch offices, she looked up at her big brother. He was fourteen years her senior and still as trim as ever.

Mitch pulled open one of the double doors and held it for Kate. She entered the welcome center and glanced around at the comfortable leather couches and chairs that surrounded a fireplace. An enormous television filled another wall. There was even a billiards table.

"Wow, you've redecorated in here."

"Yeah, tourist season will be on us before you know it. Reece likes to freshen things up once a year."

Every time she came home, she was a little surprised at what her brothers had created from nothing. Tourists came from all over the country to stay at the ranch owned by the Rainbolts. She was part of this somehow. Was this her future? Or simply a rest stop? She wasn't sure.

At the reception desk, Violet Boerner,

who managed reservations and the phones, offered an enthusiastic wave while she held a landline to her ear. Kate waved back, warmed by the gesture. Okay, maybe Rebel Ranch was the closest thing to home that she had right now. And for this haven of refuge, she was grateful.

Across the expansive room, a door opened and Reece walked out, occupied by a folder in his hands. He looked up and stopped. A grin split his face before he picked up his steps to meet her.

"Look who's finally home," he said. He took in her cast. "Ouch. I don't recall you mentioning bodily harm in your texts or calls. Not that there were many of either."

Mitch was the gentle family rock, but Reece was the no-nonsense brother who kept her grounded. Tag-team substitute parents. When he reached out to hug her, she winced at his generous embrace.

"Your shoulder hurts?" he asked.

"Oh, you know. A little muscle pain here and there."

He crossed his arms and peered down

at her, clearly ready to interrogate. Reece would be her toughest critic. He was a former rodeo cowboy, and his scrutiny would be difficult to evade.

"Where'd this happen?" His expression remained unyielding, his gaze assessing.

"Tucson Rodeo. A run-in with a frisky bull. No big deal."

"I thought the idea was to stay inside those barrels." He offered a sound of pure disgust. "Seriously, Kate, why didn't you give us a heads-up?"

"Reece, you of all people know it's the nature of the job." She turned to Mitch. "Will you back me up here? I can remember Reece coming home bruised and banged up plenty of times."

"True," Mitch said. "But he's never had as much sense as you have."

"That's not helpful," Kate muttered. Injuries were part and parcel of her career. They were well aware that she'd gone from rodeo barrel racer to rodeo clown. She was a bullfighter now, spending her time jumping in and out of barrels to protect the rodeo bull riders.

"Maybe it's time to call it quits," Reece said. "Rodeo is a young man...person's sport."

"Surely, you aren't saying I've tapped out?" she countered. "My friend Franny is as old as Mitch, and she's still in the rodeo."

"Ouch," Mitch muttered.

"Yeah, but your friend isn't sitting in barrels. Kate, I'm taking the long route to say we missed you."

His stern features softened with the admission, and Kate's throat tightened. There was nothing she could say to that. She'd missed her brothers more than ever, and the accident had only emphasized how important family was.

"Come on." Reece nodded toward the conference room.

Kate walked around the spacious room, admiring the framed photos of Rebel Ranch in various stages of development. She noted a recent photo of Ballard Farm, the property next door to their original holdings and Reece's latest project with his wife, Claire.

"Things are coming along at the farm?" she asked.

"Yep. We'll open the bed-and-breakfast in time for the Memorial Day crowd."

"Wow. That's coming up fast."

"Yeah, tell me about it. We've got a lot of the ranch finances and sweat locked into this venture."

Violet walked in a moment later with a tray that held donuts, fritters and a coffee carafe, and she gestured for Kate to sit down.

"Vi, I could've gotten that," Mitch said.

"Yes. But then I wouldn't get to say hello to my favorite Rainbolt." She reached over to give Kate a gentle embrace. "Good to see you, sweetie. If you need anything, let me know."

"I will."

"I thought I was her favorite," Mitch said when she'd left the room. He grabbed three shiny black mugs with the Rebel Ranch logo and poured coffee.

"You're her favorite old man," Reece said.

Mitch only glared back at the words and slid a mug across the table to Kate.

Kate laughed. She'd missed the teasing repartee. She took a napkin and placed a golden fritter onto a plate, wasting no time before taking a bite. "This is wonderful. Thank you."

"How long have you been on the road?" Reece asked.

"Since yesterday. I drove straight through."

"With a broken arm?" Reece blinked. "Is that even legal?"

"I checked. It's not illegal."

Reece scoffed loudly. "Come on, Kate, we would have come up and driven you home."

"That's exactly why I didn't call. I can take care of myself."

"Someday, I'm going to have that stitched on a hat for you. You've been saying it since you were a kid."

"Only because I grew up with four brothers. I had to fight for my independence."

Mitch glanced between Kate and Reece, then cleared his throat in an attempt to diffuse the situation. "How long are you staying?"

Kate sucked in a breath. "A while. If you'll have me."

Reece's brows shot up. "Whoa! Did she say what I think she said?" He looked to Mitch for confirmation.

Kate took a deep breath. "I need some time to think about the future."

"Sure. I get that," Reece said. "What are your plans?"

"You know me. No long-term plans. But you did say you needed help with the cattle expansion, so I thought…"

Panic crossed her brother's face.

"I ran into Jess McNally in town this morning," she added.

Reece cringed.

"I thought you were going to consider me for the position."

"Yeah, we were. Three months ago," Reece returned. "I practically nagged you about the job, and you never let me know if you wanted it."

Kate nodded, acknowledging that he was right. She'd waffled over the decision to move back to Rebel until the choice had been made for her, thanks to an ornery bull.

"And Jess? What happened there? You lured him down from Montana?" she asked.

"What happened? It's already April," Reece said. "You've hardly checked in the last few months, except for a quick phone message here and there." He looked at her. "Were you dodging us?"

She eyed her brother and frowned. In true Reece fashion, he'd turned the question around on her.

"I spend half my time on the road and the other half practicing. You know that," Kate returned. The words were all truth. She hadn't lied. Nor had she admitted that she had been lying low and avoiding her family while she recuperated.

"Kate," Reece continued. "We're growing faster than we can handle. I'm managing the orchards next door, and Claire is handling the Ballard Farm B&B while wrangling a three-month-old. Mitch is pretty much doing everything else on the ranch. We needed help ASAP. Believe me, it was fortunate that I ran into Jess."

"If Jess is your new foreman, where would I fit in? I mean, if I decided to make Rebel a long-term commitment."

"What do you think about equine management?" Reece asked. "I know it's not the foreman job, but you have a lot of talent that we can use." He raised a brow.

Disappointment and gratitude were her immediate thoughts. Her life was out of control, but this was something she could latch on to and ground herself with until she figured things out.

"Thank you, Reece," she murmured.

"You'd report to Jess." Reece shot her a concerned look. "Is that a problem? I know you dated a time or two, but that was a long time ago."

Kate looked away. She'd never let on to her brothers that she and Jess had dated exclusively in college. She had three big brothers who'd regularly terrified her few suitors in high school. Keeping them out of her private life was a skill she'd fine-tuned when she was a teenager.

"It's not a problem for me if it isn't for him."

"Jess assured me that you and he were long-gone history."

Good to know she wasn't even memorable after he'd asked her to marry him.

Reece peered closer. "Is that right?"

"Absolutely," she said firmly. "History. And I bet he's got a wife and a houseful of kids already."

"Not that I know of," Reece said. Again, he looked to Mitch, who offered a shake of his head.

Kate put on a smile while digesting that information with mixed emotions. "I can start in the stables tomorrow."

"Tomorrow?" Mitch released a breath. "I'm guessing there isn't much you can do with a broken arm. It's not like you'll be riding."

"What about using a mounting block?"

"Nope," Reece said. "You'll need a doctor's release form before you start working anywhere on the ranch besides desk duty."

"You must be kidding. I can remember you coming home from the Scottsdale Parada Del Sol Rodeo with a broken shoulder, and it didn't stop you from riding."

He opened his mouth, and Kate cut him off with a palm in the air before he could speak.

"Don't even think about saying it's because I'm a girl."

"Maybe it's because you're hardheaded and stubborn." He raised his brows in challenge.

"So says the king of stubborn." Kate burst out laughing and grimaced as her ribs protested the action.

Reece shook his head. "Flattery will get you nowhere. Get checked by the clinic in Rebel, and then we'll discuss how soon we can get you on the official payroll."

"You've offered me a position that I can't actually have until a doctor clears me?"

"Correct," he said with a nod.

"That's not fair," Kate muttered. She'd had enough doctor visits to last a lifetime and had a stack of bills to prove it.

"It's the best answer you'll get for now," Reece said.

"You know," Mitch began, "we should have a little get-together to welcome you home."

Kate shook her head firmly. What was there to celebrate? "I don't think—"

"Yeah, that's a great idea," Reece said to Mitch as though she wasn't there. "Kate Rainbolt is home. I'd say a little party is in order."

"Guys, really. I don't want to inconvenience you."

"Not an inconvenience. We'll have a housewarming party at your place," Mitch said.

"I don't have a place."

"Sure you do." Reece smiled. "Tucker's house is still empty. Does that work for you?"

"What would Tucker say?" she asked, almost afraid to get her hopes up. A house? She'd been living in a trailer or her truck since she left home. A house seemed too good to even dare to imagine.

"Tucker sold the place to Rebel Ranch when he and Jena got married," Mitch said.

"Oh. I didn't know that. Well, then, thank you. I'll write a check for the first month's rent as soon as I unpack my checkbook."

"Cut it out," Reece interjected. "You don't pay rent on your own land. It's one of the few perks of being part owner of the property."

"There are perks?"

"Sure," Reece said. "If all goes as planned with the launch next door, we all are finally going to see a handsome distribution check next January. That means the Rainbolts will finally see profit in their back pocket."

"I don't feel like I should get a revenue check. I don't work here."

"Doesn't matter. You're part owner of Rebel Ranch, which makes you part owner

of Ballard Farm along with the vet clinic
in town. Our holdings have grown." When
Reece looked at her, a wide grin lit up his
face. "You know, there's one more perk I'd
nearly forgotten."

"What's that?"

"Luna Diaz is the ranch chef. She'll be
thrilled to cater your welcome-home party."

Kate quickly shook her head. "No. No. I
don't think a party is a good idea."

"He didn't mean party," Mitch said. "A
little get-together with family and friends.
Let us do this, Kate. We want to welcome
you home, proper-like." Her eldest brother
smiled, making it impossible to say no.

"Okay, all right. A few people. Um,
when?"

"Next Saturday night work for you?"

"Fine." She finished off her fritter and
eyed a second one. "Mind if I take a few
of these with me?"

Reece laughed. "I'll have someone run
them over to your new home."

Her new home. There was something ex-
citing and terrifying about unpacking for

the long haul. It was discomfiting to return to Oklahoma with nothing but her few possessions and her horse. She'd been so idealistic when she'd left ten years ago. Now it seemed the prodigal cowgirl had returned a failure.

"Thanks," Kate murmured, humbled by the offer. "I really appreciate this."

"Stop acting like you're a houseguest," Reece said. His voice held a raw edge. "You're family, Kate. We lost Levi, but we still have each other."

She nodded as emotion washed over her at the mention of her little brother, Levi. The auto accident that took his life was six years ago, but the pain remained a constant ache.

"I'll send someone over to help you unload," Reece said.

"I don't need—"

Reece narrowed his gaze, shutting down the rest of her response.

Kate raised her palms. "All I have is a half-dozen boxes."

Mitch looked at his brother. "She'll need furniture and a bed."

"Got it covered," Reece said with a snap of his fingers. "We've got furniture in storage in the attic here. And I can take a bed from a guest suite upstairs."

"Thank you so much, guys."

"We're just happy that you're home," Reece said.

"Me too," she said. "So, what's on the agenda for today?"

"Not a thing for you. We'll talk tomorrow," Mitch said. "In the meantime, I'll have someone drop off groceries later today."

"That's not necessary."

"You have to eat." Mitch offered a tender smile. "Now quit protesting. We're your big brothers. Deal with it."

She leaned back in the chair, grateful and suddenly very weary. Her arm and rib cage throbbed. Elevating the extremity and applying an ice pack would help, along with some over-the-counter analgesic tablets.

Maybe taking it easy today was a good idea. She looked forward to a hot shower and a nap. Then she'd sit down and figure out a plan to stall her creditors until she got a doctor's clearance and her brothers were willing to put her on the payroll.

The accident had lassoed her into a hefty medical-bill payment plan, and the next installment was due soon. Though that bit of information was something she'd keep to herself. There was no way she'd allow her brothers to bail her out when it was her poor decisions that had put her square in the middle of a life turned upside down.

"Are we good?" Reece asked.

Kate glanced at both of her brothers. "Yes. We're good."

Good until she could think straight and figure out what the future held for a broken-down cowgirl who'd gone from riding a horse to riding a desk.

Jess pulled up to the modest brick-and-clapboard ranch home with a white picket fence. Kate was so not a white-picket-fence woman.

As he parked the Double R pickup, it occurred to him that he'd made an assumption he had no right to make. They'd dated in college. On graduation day, they'd saluted the future. He with a ranch-operations degree in his hand and Kate with a degree in business administration, per Mitch's edict that she attend college. That was the day that Jess had proposed marriage. Things hadn't worked out as well as he'd hoped. Kate had burned rubber leaving Rebel. Leaving him.

Back then, Jess's situation at home hadn't looked any better. His father hadn't had a good word to say to him after he'd changed his major from premed. The old man had wanted Jess to follow his footsteps into medicine. The rift between them had only widened over time. His father's sudden death last year meant Jess would never have a chance to make things right.

Now, here he was, back in Rebel ashamed

of himself and determined to be there for his ailing mother.

"You sure are thinking awful hard."

"What?" Jess turned in the truck's seat to face Willard Cornell, the wily hand who was older than dirt and told everyone so any chance he got.

"I'd say you were in your happy place, 'cept you sure weren't smiling."

"It's Thursday," Jess said. "I always think on Thursday. That frees me up to daydream on Friday."

"Tell me another story," Willard said. "I don't think you're a daydreamer at all. I've had my eye on you since you started at Rebel Ranch. You're so pragmatic it scares me."

"Pragmatic? There's a two-dollar word."

"If the boot fits." Willard nodded to the house in front of them. "What do you think about Miss Kate's return?"

"I don't think about it."

"So you say." Willard removed his battered hat, slapped it on his thigh and covered his gray head again. "I remember when Reece started things out here. All we had was a few horses. That boy had a few stops and starts back then. He didn't even realize that Rebel Ranch could be a tourist attraction until a few more years down the road when he got his life straightened out."

He eyed Jess and kept talking. "I was one of the first hires at Rebel Ranch. Miss Kate was at college. She came home some weekends, and as I recall, you followed her around more than a few times."

Jess pushed open the door of the truck, annoyed at the memory of how naive he'd been in those days. Naive enough to give away his heart. "I didn't follow her around," he said. "And we were kids. Haven't been a kid in a long time."

Willard laughed as he too got out of the truck. "Yeah, right, 'cause you're all of what? Thirty?"

"Thirty-one."

"Ha," Willard scoffed. "I was twice as old as you when I was your age."

"I believe it."

"So you headed to Montana right after college?" Willard asked.

Jess lowered the truck's gate and grabbed two brown bags from the Piggly Wiggly. "You sure are nosy," he said.

"That's 'cause you never say two words."

"Maybe you should take a hint."

"Not me. Takes a two-by-four for me to take a hint."

"That's nothing to be proud of," Jess said.

"Are you going to answer the question?"

"Yeah, I had an opportunity on a ranch in Billings. No big deal."

"And now you're back."

"That's right. Can you grab that other bag of groceries?" Jess asked. He reached for his toolbox with his free hand and strode to the front door.

Before he had a chance to put down the toolbox and knock, the door swung open, and he faced Kate through the screen. She stood to the side and eyed him, clearly not pleased to find him on her stoop. Her long hair, the color of dark chocolate, was pulled into a knot at the top of her head. The ends were dark purple, as though they'd been dipped in paint, no doubt a salute to her rebel nature. In a short-sleeved T-shirt and yoga pants, she looked good. Way too good.

Jess reminded himself to focus. He had no business noticing how Kate Rainbolt looked, nor should he care.

"We meet again," she said. "How may I help you?"

"Willard and I are here to get things moved into the house."

She offered a resigned sigh. "Come on in."

When he slipped past her into the foyer, the scent of mangoes tickled his nose—Kate's shampoo. The scent took him places he'd long forgotten and he froze.

"What's wrong?" she asked.

"Nothing." Not a thing, except he didn't want to be thinking about the scent of mangoes.

It was when she turned to face him that Jess saw the long cast on her left arm. How had he missed that this morning? Maybe because she had wanted him to miss it.

"You broke your arm?" he asked.

"Looks like." Her stance said she wouldn't be entertaining any questions on the subject.

"Where do you want these groceries, Miss Kate?" Willard said from behind him.

"Oh, Willard. Thank you. The kitchen is right through there." She offered a generous and welcoming smile to the old cowboy.

Willard looked Jess up and down. "You gonna just stand there?"

Jess followed him into the kitchen, biting back a comment.

"Looking as pretty as ever, Miss Kate," Willard observed. "How'd you bust up your arm?"

"An ugly bull decided he liked me better in the dirt than standing up."

"Maybe it was the same bull that chewed off my digits." Willard held up his right hand, where he was missing two fingers.

Jess's lips twitched. Another day and another tall tale about how Willard had lost his fingers a few years back. In six weeks, he'd already heard six stories. No doubt the real story was much less colorful.

Laughter slipped from Kate's mouth at the old cowboy's words, and for a moment, she relaxed, reminding him of the girl he used to know.

"Can I get you two something to drink? Or maybe an apple fritter?" she asked.

"Sure," Willard said with a grin.

Jess held out an arm before Willard could pass by. "Let's get the stuff in the back of the truck emptied first."

"Well, you're no fun," Willard grumbled.

"That's why they hired me," Jess returned.

An hour later, Willard continued to grumble as he closed up the back of the pickup and dusted off his hands. "Now can we take a break?"

"Not until we get that bed frame set up."

A phone buzzed, and Willard pulled a cell from his pocket. "From the boss."

"Which boss?" Jess asked.

"Reece. He needs me over at Ballard Farm." Willard looked up at Jess. "Think you can handle that bed frame all by your lonesome?"

Jess tossed him the keys to the ranch truck. "I'll walk back."

"Where's your buddy?" Kate asked when he stepped into the house.

When she smiled, Jess looked away. He wouldn't be caught in the snare of those blue eyes.

"Reece needed him," he said. Grabbing the toolbox from the floor, he headed down the hall, growing more annoyed that he was now alone with Kate. He was supposed to be a foreman, not her personal mover or the local handyman. What happened to avoiding the woman? Her brothers weren't making that easy.

"You don't need to do that," she called after him.

Jess stopped and turned around. Kate's eyes rounded as she too stopped.

"I'm employed by Rebel Ranch. Your brothers asked me to make sure you're set up here. If you have a problem with that, take it up with them, Miss Rainbolt."

"So that's how it's going to be?" she returned with her right hand on her hip.

"Just doing my job." Jess did an about-face and headed into the master bedroom. Kate was the boss's sister and a distraction he didn't need. He took the metal-frame segments and attached the wheels and feet. Then he added the center support beam and positioned it with the frame segments. Twice they slipped out of place.

Kate stepped into the room and knelt down. "Look, this is as awkward for me as it is for you." She held the sidearm segment nearest to the door for him. "And I'll level with you. I came home thinking I'd have a shot at the foreman position. Maybe stick around for a while. I was surprised to find out you got the job."

Jess stared at her for a long moment. He didn't know which bit of information surprised him more. The fact that she came home thinking she'd be foreman or the idea that she might stick around. He pulled a screwdriver out of the toolbox and set to work, attaching all the segments. It would have been nice if Mitch or Reece had given him a heads-up that she'd been offered the position first.

"I wasn't aware of the situation," Jess finally said. He took a deep breath. "With ten years of experience and a degree in ranch operations, I've proven that I'm up to the task." He didn't know why he should have to defend himself, but there it was on the table.

"Are you saying I can't?" Kate asked.

"Not with that arm, you can't."

"Reece plans to give me the opportunity to handle the equine side when I'm cleared for riding. Reporting to you."

There was a long silence between them.

"I'm guessing there's a question in there somewhere," he finally said.

"Do you think we can find a way to work together?" Kate asked.

"Absolutely. We've both moved on." He answered without hesitation, though his brain was racing with serious doubts. "But

I'd appreciate it if you'd remember that I applied for the job without knowing you wanted it too."

"Fair enough," she said.

Jess stood, grabbed the headboard, and slid the legs into place. He looked over at Kate. "Is this where you want it?"

She nodded.

He grabbed the box springs and then the mattress and slid them on the frame. "You're all set."

"Thanks."

"How are you going to make the bed with your arm?"

"I'll manage. I've become adept at working with one hand."

He eyed her, knowing he shouldn't prolong the conversation, but curiosity won out. "How'd it happen?"

"The usual. An arena accident." She glanced away as she said the words, which made him suspect there was much more to the story than Kate was telling. Still, it didn't matter. It wasn't any of his business. He was the foreman of Rebel Ranch, hired to do a job, and he wouldn't feel guilty about that.

Bottom line was, he was here because his mother needed him, and he would not let her down. This time, Jess wasn't going to walk away from his troubles. Kate Rainbolt didn't figure into the equation.

All he had to do was stay out of her way, because this morning when their gazes had collided in the donut shop, he'd come to the alarming conclusion that after ten years, Kate still had the power to make his brain disengage in less than sixty seconds.

In that instant, he'd made a decision that there was no way he would be collateral damage when she rode off into the sunset once more. Because it wasn't a matter of if she would ride away, it was a matter of when.

Chapter Two

Kate crossed the gravel yard in long strides. Timing was everything, and according to the schedule she'd glimpsed in the barn, her brothers didn't work on Sunday. Jess was on duty every other Sunday. Not today.

As she approached the barn, Willard exited with his familiar bowlegged swagger. "Miss Kate, afternoon." He tipped his hat and grinned. "Can I help you with anything, ma'am?"

"Oh, no. I'm getting a little exercise."

"Nice day for a walk," he said with a glance at the dusky skies overhead. "Though it's supposed to rain later."

"Not until tonight. I checked."

"That so?" He gave a slow shake of his head. "Never can trust those weather fellas. They say sunshine and you find yourself in the middle of a gully washer."

"So true." She smiled and kept walking, praying he'd head in the other direction.

Rounding the corner of the barn, she peeked back. Willard was halfway across the yard already. Kate checked to be sure no one was around before she approached the far side of the structure where two ranch UTVs were usually parked.

Sure enough, they were there waiting for her, one bright green and the other blue. Both had the keys inside. She chose the blue one because the door enclosures had been removed and she was ready for the wind to blow through her hair. She'd been inside most of the time since she'd arrived Thursday, setting up the house and growing antsier by the minute.

The church service this morning had been the highlight of her week, and that might be fine any other time, but her bruised tailbone had protested that the church pew's polished oak was much too hard for extended sitting. She'd focused on her Bible and tried to ignore the discomfort as well as the fact that Jess sat across the aisle from her.

It was Jess she hoped to avoid now as she turned the key in the ignition of the UTV. She'd learned to sweet-talk her brothers and get her way at an early age. Jess, however, saw right through her. Dealing with him wouldn't be quite as easy.

Rebel Ranch was a big place, though, and with a little careful planning, she hoped that she could avoid him indefinitely. The idea of staying one step ahead of the ranch foreman made her chuckle with giddy satisfaction.

Fastening the harness seat belt carefully over her bruised rib cage, Kate again checked the sky, ever vigilant during tornado season for unexpected changes in the weather. But the sky remained the same dusky gray, heavy and full with the anticipation of evening thunderstorms, just as her weather app promised.

Rain. The thought buoyed her spirits.

There was nothing better than sleeping with the window cracked as a cool breeze fluttered the curtains. The sound of rain tapping against the windowpane provided a lullaby for sleep. Sleep that had eluded her for weeks.

When the UTV sputtered a few times as she drove over the red-clay trail to the back of the ranch, Kate's glance went to the gas tank. It was full, so she kept going, trying to avoid the jarring rough tracks on the ground. The doctors told her it would take one to two months to heal her ribs. When the vehicle hit another bump, she realized they were healing…just much slower than she would have liked.

A breeze picked up, and she imagined herself riding Einstein as she passed a herd of cattle. The wind danced in and out of the vehicle, kissing her face and whipping her hair into a frenzy.

Kate guided the UTV up and over a hill to a thick circle of loblolly pines.

There it was. Reece's spot. She parked the vehicle close to the conifers and grabbed her water bottle and sweatshirt. Her boots crunched on dead leaves and pine needles that blanketed the ground beneath the trees until she came to a grassy clearing where a creek welcomed her with soft burbles of water tumbling over the shale. She sat on the edge of the stream and pulled off her boots. Cold water teased her toes and bubbled past in a race to the rocks downstream.

Kate tucked her sweatshirt beneath her to cushion her sore body from the hard ground. As the wind teased her hair and the scent of pine danced around her, she whispered a small thanks to God that she was alive. The last few weeks had been brutal. Now that her sutures were healing and the bruises across her back and side had faded along with some of her nightmares, she was beginning to feel whole again.

Was it time to stop chasing the rodeo?

The end of life on the circuit meant closing the door on the search for her father. Mitch always said that TJ Rainbolt wasn't to blame for their situation. Their mother, Margaret Katherine, had passed, and TJ had panicked. He'd been a good old boy who couldn't figure out how he had ended up with five kids or what to do with them. So he'd walked away.

At eight years old, Kate had been the apple of her daddy's eye, and she'd been certain she could convince him to come back if she only had a chance. She'd been to almost every rodeo town, big and small, west of the Mississippi during her career, and she'd never found the man who had been her hero growing up.

The plan was to find him and show him that she was good enough. Good enough to rodeo, just like him. Good enough to deserve his love.

Kate bit back emotion. She'd failed all the way around.

The wind shifted, and Kate tensed, searching the sky. A native Okie, she knew to stay alert for spring tornados, but the threatening dark clouds on the horizon said thunderstorms, not twisters. When a flash of pink-and-yellow light darted across the sky, followed by a low boom, Kate scrambled to grab her boots. She nearly toppled over in an awkward attempt to get them on with one hand and managed to jar her tender rib cage in the process.

When lightning again zipped across the sky, chased by thunder that sounded way too close, she picked up her boots and sweatshirt and dashed across the dry pine needles through the trees to the UTV. Leaves whirled as the wind tossed them into the air, and the giant loblollies shuddered.

She slid into the vehicle and wiped the needles and dirt off her feet before shoving them into the boots. A determined gust of wind blew through, making Kate regret not taking the UTV with doors and windows. At least this one had a roof.

For a moment, she sat very still, catching her breath while the pain in her middle subsided. When the rain began to patter against the hood and the roof, she pulled the keys out of her pocket and slid them into the ignition. The UTV jumped to life and then promptly died.

"Noooo," she muttered. Kate tried again, her gaze landing on the gas gauge. *Empty?* That was impossible. It had been full. She was sure of it.

As if unable to hold back a moment longer, the skies opened up and the pattering became a deluge. The wind slanted the rain toward the driver's side of the vehicle, making her easy prey for the stinging moisture. Kate slid to the passenger side and huddled near the edge of the seat.

Thunder crashed once more, and she shivered.

"I need a plan," she said aloud. "I can call my brothers and be humiliated, or..." Or she could wait out the storm and walk back. Of course it would be dark by the time she returned to the house. Walking through the pastures at night was never wise. The ground was uneven, and she'd likely step into a hole and turn her ankle. Then there was her cast, which wasn't supposed to get wet.

She pulled out her phone. One bar. Calling for help wasn't going to happen.

It was entirely possible that a man on a horse would appear out of nowhere and save her. Maybe one wearing a black hat and duster, with his collar pulled up. He'd smile and whisk her into his arms, and they'd ride his stallion back to the ranch, racing the storm and winning.

Kate began to laugh, eyes watering with amusement. Her sense of humor saved her at every turn.

As she peered through the windshield, a drop of water landed with a plop on her face. Kate wiped the moisture from her cheek and examined the interior ceiling of the vehicle. A burgeoning drop was suspended above her head. She held her sweatshirt to the spot.

In the distance, the sound of an engine could be heard over the din of the falling rain. A minute later, she was surprised to see the bright green Rebel Ranch UTV pull up next to her. Someone got out and dashed through the rain to her vehicle. He slid into the driver's seat.

Jess McNally. Her unlikely hero.

Kate laughed.

"I'm glad you think this is funny." Jess pushed back the brim of his hat and offered her a view of his rain-dampened face. He wasn't happy, and the gray eyes were as dark as the sky outside as he stared at her. "Next time you decide to drive off into a storm, could you do it on someone else's shift?"

Kate straightened in her seat, automatically preparing to cross her arms. Until the cast got in her way. Then a drop of rain splashed on her face, completely destroying her attempts at an indignant stance. She swiped at the moisture.

"Nothing to say?" he asked.

"Why are you here? You're off today. I saw the schedule."

"I traded with one of the wranglers. His wife is having a baby."

She frowned, irritation rising. So she'd gotten stuck in a storm. What was the big deal?

"How did you know I was out here?" she finally asked.

"Willard saw you around the barn, and then the UTV went missing. It was an easy jump to big trouble."

"Thanks a lot. For your information, there's something wrong with the gas gauge."

"I know. It sticks. You probably ran out of gas."

"That's not my fault. And I'd like to remind you that you didn't have to come out here and find me. You aren't responsible for anything to do with me."

"I won't turn the other way when I see you in distress."

"In distress?" She gaped at him. "I am not in distress."

He frowned. "From where I'm sitting, it sure looks like you could use some assistance."

She sat silently, watching the rivulets of

rain on the windshield. There was nothing to say. If it were anyone else, she would be grateful. But it was Jess, and at every turn, he saw her mess up, driving back home the fact that she was a failure.

"Why are you so annoyed?" he asked. "I'm the one who's going to be called on the carpet if anything happens to you when I'm in charge."

Even as she silently denied the accusation, she knew that he was right. She was annoyed. Not at him but at herself for looking foolish in front of him.

"So now what?" she asked.

"Let's get into the other vehicle." He pulled off his barn coat and handed it to her. "Here. Wrap this around your cast."

"Thank you," she murmured.

Jess held the door as she slid across the seat and hopped from one UTV to the other. She cringed in pain as both her arm and her ribs were jostled by the movement. By the time Jess got in the driver's seat next to her, he was soaked.

"You're all wet," she said, stating the

obvious. The soaked denim shirt with its Western yoke only emphasized his broad shoulders. Kate looked away.

"I won't melt," he said. "How about you?"

"I'm fine." She unwrapped her arm and handed him back his jacket.

Tossing the coat into the back of the vehicle, Jess turned the key in the ignition and jacked up the heater until it blasted warm air.

Overhead, another crack of lightning filled the sky, followed by a thunderous reverberation that promised more was on the way.

Kate gripped the door handle and prayed it would stop. Within minutes, the rain had increased from a downpour to a slanted sheet of deluge.

"This is just great," Jess muttered. "We'll have to wait it out. I'm not going to drive in a storm when there's no visibility."

The silence between them only widened as the rain hammered the vehicle.

"How long did you say you're staying?" Jess asked.

She jerked her head around at his tone. "Why do you say it like that?"

Jess shrugged. "Merely acknowledging that you don't sit still long."

"You don't know that." His words stung, and it stuck in her craw that he could still get into her head.

"You've been on the circuit for ten years. Like a tumbleweed." He shrugged once again. "It is what it is."

"What it is, is the nature of the work. Besides, I told you in college that I had a mission. You didn't get it back then. I guess some things never change."

"Are you still looking for your father?"

Kate tensed at his words. "It doesn't matter." Maybe it did, but she was not going to discuss TJ Rainbolt with him.

"No?" he asked softly.

"No. What matters is that I haven't decided what I'm going to do with the rest of my life, so I don't know how long I'll be here." She looked at him. "I imagine you have everything in your world figured out, as usual, all nice and neat and tied with a bow." Kate's gaze skimmed over his profile and then away. He probably had a five-year plan too.

She bristled at the thought that even though years had passed, Jess still possessed way too many of her secrets. He was the only person who knew the real reason she'd first headed out to the circuit to become a professional barrel racer. Kate regretted sharing that information.

"When did you say you landed in Rebel?" she asked.

"Six weeks ago. When I took the position here at the ranch. Why?"

She shrugged. "Just making conversation."

His expression said he doubted that.

"What made you leave Montana?" she asked.

Jess frowned. "How did you know I was in Montana?"

"Someone must have mentioned it." She recalled overhearing only bits of a conversation when she was in town for Tucker's wedding.

For a very long minute, they were silent. The only sound between them the rain, which had slowed to a rooftop drumming.

Jess ran a hand over his face. "I came back because my mother is having some health challenges."

Kate released a small gasp. Her heart took the full brunt of his words. "I'm so sorry," she murmured. She genuinely liked Jess's mother, who had been childhood friends with her own mother. Without thinking, Kate placed her hand on his and then froze, realizing what she'd done.

Jess's startled gray eyes met hers, and he shifted away from the contact.

"We better get back," he said, his face still without expression. "I told my mother I'd stop by this afternoon to visit. Some days are harder than others since my father passed."

His father. Out of the blue, a memory came roaring back of Jess's dad, Dr. Jacob McNally, when she'd run into him in town that last year of college. *You'll never be good enough for my son. It would be best*

*if you walk away right now before things
get complicated.*

He was right. So she had walked away
and not looked back.

For the second time in less than a week,
she found herself thinking about what-
ifs—questioning the decision to leave ten
years ago. Kate pushed the thoughts away
as fast as she could. She wasn't ready to
open that particular Pandora's box just yet.

The unmistakable clanging sound of a
rig pulling onto the ranch road had Jess
stepping out of the stables to see what was
going on.

Kate stood in the drive, grinning, as an
older woman jumped down from a dually
that pulled a gooseneck trailer and greeted
Kate with enthusiastic but careful hugs.

The trailer door creaked when the women
opened the back. Jess moved forward to
offer his assistance with the horse and
froze. After yesterday's UTV rain adven-
ture, he wasn't quite sure where he stood
with Kate. It seemed like a case of one step

forward and two back, which wasn't exactly a renewed friendship. He sensed it wouldn't take much from either of them to kick up a disagreement.

Nope, he'd stay right where he was for the time being.

As Kate and her horse enjoyed a reunion, the lanky middle-aged woman with a straw cowboy hat walked toward him. "You must be one of Kate's brothers." She offered a hand, which Jess took.

"Jess McNally, ranch foreman. Pleased to meet you, ma'am."

"Ah, sorry. You were watching Kate like someone who cares. I thought..."

Jess dismissed the words immediately. "Everyone here cares about Kate," he returned.

The woman nodded. "I'm Franny Cox. Kate and I have road-tripped together on the circuit the last few years."

"You live in Oklahoma?" he asked.

"Texas."

Jess clucked his tongue. "That's too bad."

Franny laughed. "Spoken like a true Okie."

Both of them turned to watch Kate whisper in the gelding's ear, all the while stroking his neck and running a loving hand over his flank.

"She sure loves that horse," Jess said.

"Einstein? Yeah, she does." Franny smiled. "Kate looks better. I'm glad she came home. Though I knew she'd make it through the other side of this. Kate's a fighter."

"What exactly happened in Tucson?" The question was out of his mouth before he could decide if he really wanted to hear the answer. Yet he had to know.

"She didn't tell you?"

"Kate's as tight-lipped as they come."

Franny eyed him warily, then she shrugged. "She'll give me a dressing down, but the fact is, the accident is public knowledge. There was a front-page write-up in the local Tucson paper."

Accident? Write-up in the paper? Jess found himself tensing at Franny's ominous words. Kate's dismissive remarks had led him to believe her injury was incidental. No big deal.

"The last night of the Tucson Rodeo," Franny continued. "A bull nearly killed a rider. If it wasn't for Kate's quick thinking, the ornery beast would have. Kate got stomped on for her troubles." Franny blinked and swallowed hard, putting a hand to her chest. "Seeing her taken from that arena on a stretcher nearly stopped my heart."

Jess closed his eyes for a moment as a visual of the scene that Franny described flashed before him. A physical pain gutted him as he imagined Kate lying in the dirt, like a broken rag doll.

"When was this?" His voice came out uneven and raw.

"February."

"February?" Jess counted back the weeks. "Where has she been since then?"

"Tucson. She had two surgeries on her arm."

"Two?"

"Yeah, I don't know the details, and of course, Kate won't elaborate none. She rented a studio apartment, and I checked in on her between rodeos and took care of her horse."

The object of their discussion turned and eyed them, her face dark with suspicion. "What are you two talking about?"

"The weather," Jess called. There was no way Kate would tolerate his pity, and the look she shot him as she led her horse into the stables told him as much.

"Uh-oh," Franny said. "Do me a favor and don't mention this. She's got this idea about not being a burden to her family."

"I won't." He turned to step away and then paused. "Thanks for taking care of Kate, Franny. I know her brothers would want to thank you, as well."

"Taking care of Kate was the easy part," Franny said. "Between you and me, I love her like the little sister I never had. She's always been a scrapper, trying to prove herself." The woman shook her head. "When that bull laid her out, I was terrified, because for the first time since I've known Kate, she didn't fight back."

Yeah, that scared him, as well. More than he was willing to admit.

An hour later, Jess walked from the main house toward the stables, noting that Franny's truck and trailer were gone.

When he stepped through the oversize doors of the building, the first thing he spotted was Kate saddling up the silky chestnut gelding in the aisle outside an empty stall. His heart jumped to his throat. "What are you doing?"

Kate didn't turn at his voice. At five foot seven, she was slim and tall. Her ponytail swayed back and forth as she adjusted the stirrups. "What does it look like I'm doing?"

"How did you even get that saddle on him?"

"That's a secret."

Her chin was set with determination, and he weighed whether he wanted to be the one to poke the bear.

When she rubbed the horse gently behind

the ears, he whinnied. "Einstein wants to know if you have places to be."

"Nowhere at the moment."

"That's too bad." Kate grimaced as she pushed a mounting block into position next to Einstein.

"Hang on," he said. "I'll help you."

She waved him away with her free hand. "You're not always going to be around. I need to do this myself."

"I was thinking about Einstein."

"Einstein is obedient. He wouldn't move if I lit a firecracker, which is why he and I work so well together. Mutual respect." She patted the animal's flank. "Right, boy?"

"I don't think that's…"

His voice trailed off when Kate stepped onto the block, swayed and waved her arm as she began to fall backward.

Jess rushed forward and grabbed her. The moment his hands spanned her waist, she cried out in pain.

He set her on the ground and stepped away while trying to figure out what had just happened. Kate released tight, shaky breaths and leaned over, her hand on her thigh.

"What was that?" Jess asked.

"I don't know," she said. Her flustered voice matched how unnerved he felt at the moment.

"You don't know?"

"Sometimes....sometimes I randomly seem to lose my balance." Kate looked up at him, her face pale and her breathing still unsteady.

Then he realized what was going on. He'd grown up as a doctor's kid and spent time in the Rebel Clinic. That had necessitated a few first aid classes along the way. His rudimentary diagnostic skills told him that Kate probably had a concussion and at least a few cracked ribs. That was why she'd cried out when he grabbed her.

"You're a hot mess," he muttered.

"Thanks for the pep talk."

"You really were dodging a bull. What happened to barrel racing?"

"I was barrel racing for a while. But

there's no regular paycheck unless you're a top rider. I'm good, but good doesn't pay the bills. A friend got me a referral to clown school in Reno. Turns out I'm very good at that. Even better at bullfighting."

Jess blinked. "Bullfighting?"

"Yes, sometimes I sit inside the barrel. Other times I run around distracting them, keeping the riders safe."

He let out a frustrated breath. "I know how it works. What I don't understand is why you would want to do it."

"I just told you. I'm very good, and it was a regular check."

Jess clenched and unclenched his fists as he did his best to process what she'd said. The words couldn't have been clearer, yet it still made no sense why she'd put herself at risk.

Pinning her with his gaze, he picked his way through her armor until he figured out what was going on. "Your brothers don't know how badly you were injured."

A statement. Not a question, and she stared at him. He sensed the moment she chose not to deny the words. Her shoulders relaxed, and she took a deep breath.

"No. And I don't want them to know." Her gaze pleaded with him. "You can't tell them either."

Jess didn't know what to say. Kate was a smart woman, had been top of her class in college. She'd never been an adrenaline junkie, so why was she taking chances with her life like this? The image of her broken and hurting cut through him.

"Stop thinking so loud," she said.

"What is it you think I'm thinking, Kate?"

"You're feeling sorry for me, and the last thing I need is pity."

"I don't feel sorry for you. I'm concerned." He paused. "Have you talked to anyone about what happened?"

Kate jerked back. "What? You think I need therapy?"

"You've been traumatized." Maybe a therapist could help her sort things out. Like maybe what was driving her. What had been driving her all these years.

She shook her head. "Look, it was an accident. I'm recovering. End of story."

"Are you going back?"

"You mean, to the rodeo?" She cocked her head as if wondering why he'd asked.

"Yeah, to the rodeo."

"I don't know, Jess. I don't know a lot of things right now."

He assessed her as she stood there with one arm casted and the other wrapped around her rib cage protectively. Jess wanted to understand, but it made no sense. "You're going to have to tell your brothers eventually."

"The doctors are pleased with my progress, so I don't see any reason to worry my family. They've been through enough. Things are looking up for everyone. I'll share with them on a need-to-know basis." Kate stared him down, long and hard. "I'm home, and I'm going to be fine." She licked her lips. "Do you understand?"

"I won't lie for you, Kate." Fact was, he wasn't sure he shouldn't head to Reece's office and tell him right now. This wasn't a little secret. This was Kate's life, and he didn't want to be responsible for it. Nope, he hadn't signed up for that.

"I'm not asking you to lie, Jess."

"Great, and in the meantime, you shouldn't be riding."

"Says who?"

"Anyone with eyes or a lick of common sense." He shook his head, trying to sort everything out. "You aren't even wearing a helmet."

"Okay, that is a valid point," she said. "Next time, I'll wear a helmet."

"No next time." He narrowed his gaze and assessed her. "Did your brothers okay riding?"

"I don't need their approval. I'm not a kid anymore." Kate's lips became a firm line as she inhaled and exhaled in measured breaths. "Besides, it's my horse."

"My stables." He crossed his arms. For the first time in his life, he had the upper hand with Kate, and it wasn't too bad a feeling. Except there was nothing to gloat about, because the woman was in a bad way and too stubborn to admit it.

"I have to exercise Einstein."

"I'll do that for you."

"I can walk him around," Kate protested.

"You prefer that I don't handle your horse?"

"I didn't say that."

A cell phone buzzed, and he pulled his from his pocket. "It's Reece. I've got a meeting in five minutes."

"Remember what you just promised."

"I didn't promise anything, though I've got better things to do than report to your brothers what you're up to." He paused. "Unless it involves the livestock or the horses."

"They're Rainbolt livestock and horses, which technically means they're mine," she said.

If the situation wasn't serious, he'd have himself a good laugh at that comment, but Jess knew if he gave Kate an inch, she'd take the entire horse and ride off on it. He weighed his response instead.

"*Technically*, my first obligation is to Rebel Ranch."

"If you're trying to get rid of me, it won't work," she huffed. "As soon as I can, I'll be in this barn, managing the horses."

"Reporting to me until you ride off into the sunset again."

His response seemed to only infuriate her, though he wasn't telling her something new.

"I'm not the enemy," he finally said after she'd fumed for a few minutes.

She glared at him, clearly certain of the opposite.

No, he wasn't the enemy, but if Kate Rainbolt wasn't going to be smart enough to take care of herself, he wasn't going to just stand by and let her get hurt.

Jess turned on his heel and left the stables, shaking his head. No way around it. His brain told him that Kate was trouble at every turn, and his heart agreed. Things were not going to end well.

Chapter Three

Jess stood outside the little house and hesitated. The last place he wanted to be was in the same room with Kate. Since their conversation on Monday, they'd had an unspoken pact to avoid each other. He'd seen her at a distance and made an effort to keep away from the stables, assigning Willard to monitor the equine staff.

Kate was not only a danger to herself but also a danger to him on all levels. She was a long time from being healthy enough to handle the horses. He'd deal with that when it came up and prayed that for now, a house party was the sole thing that he had to worry about.

The main reason he stood on her stoop tonight was because his bosses, *all of them*, had insisted. If the Rainbolts continued to multiply, he wasn't sure how many people he would be taking orders from soon.

He moved the gift in his left hand to his right and stared at the silver ribbon. His sister, Nicole, had assured him it was an "appropriate" housewarming gift, though he hadn't actually asked her what it was. He assumed it was something from her pottery shop. Both he and Kate would be surprised when she opened it.

The front door swung open, and he stared at Kate. This was the second time she'd surprised him before he'd had a chance to knock.

"I thought you weren't coming. Mitch just asked where you were."

He gave her a covert assessment. She wore snug dark slacks and a silky blouse with a scarf around her neck. The peachy colors suited the shiny dark hair that tumbled around her shoulders. His quick glance turned into an appreciative gaze, and he had to look away.

"Are you coming in?" she asked.

"Excuse me," he asked, distracted. "What did you say?"

"Mitch is looking for you."

"Yeah, right. Mitch. I'll do the cursory walk around the room and leave. No worries."

"Jess. We're both adults. It's only a few hours. I think we can manage. After all, look how well we've avoided each other this week." She paused. "Though I noticed your spy, Willard, checking on me when he thought I wasn't looking."

She was right on all counts, though he wouldn't admit it. Instead, he met her gaze.

Kate smiled and pushed open the door. "Come on in. Your henchman is already here."

His lips twitched at her words. "This is for you." Jess offered her the package, and their hands collided. Kate stepped back as if struck by an electric shock. The scarf around her neck slipped free and fell to the ground, and Jess scooped it up. He straightened and saw a crooked red suture line at her clavicle that the scrap of silk had hidden.

It was all he could do not to reach out to touch her, but he was torn between anger and fear. That laceration had been much too close to her carotid artery.

"Stop staring," she murmured.

"I can't help it. An inch higher and..."

"But it wasn't an inch higher, and that's what matters." She circled the scarf around her neck and crossed the ends to cover up the suture line once again.

"Kate, Franny told me."

When she sucked in a sharp breath, he realized what was going on. "Your brothers really don't know how serious the accident was, do they?" he asked.

"I don't want to talk about it, Jess."

He wasn't going to spoil the night, so he said nothing further, all the while recalling Franny Cox's words. Kate had come much closer to death than she was ready to admit. He gave himself a mental shake, reminding himself that this was none of his business, hadn't been for a long time, and his concern was misplaced.

"What's in the box?" Kate asked as he handed it to her again.

"It's a housewarming gift."

Kate's eyes warmed, and her mouth turned up with a soft smile. "Thank you. I'm not sure why everyone keeps bringing me gifts. The prodigal daughter returns. Not exactly something to celebrate."

"Sometimes it's not about us, though, is it?"

She frowned and met his gaze. "Yes. You're right."

"Careful there. You might make my head swell."

"I doubt that," she said. "May I open this now?"

"Yeah, sure."

As her fingers slid beneath the paper, he prayed his sister hadn't let him down. Kate unfolded the flap of the white box inside the decorative wrapping and lifted one of two identical mugs from the tissue. The glazed stoneware was a rich shade of coral melding into black at the base.

"These are lovely," Kate breathed. She looked up at him. "Southwest colors too. I love them. Thank you."

"My sister has a small shop in town tucked next to the bookstore."

"What? Last I heard, Nicole was headed to medical school."

"Nope. She wanted nothing to do with medicine. She's a schoolteacher. Part-time, anyhow, and she runs the shop with my mother."

"Oh, my. Your father couldn't have been happy. Both you and your sister refused to go to medical school?" Then her eyes rounded, and she released a small gasp. "I'm so sorry. You've lost your father, and here I am speaking ill of him."

"You're not saying anything that isn't true." What did it say about his family that the thing Kate remembered was that his father was an unyielding man who sought to control everything?

"Tell Nicole thank you," Kate said.

"I will. I'm glad you like it."

Kate started toward the house and then stopped and turned. "How's your mother doing? You mentioned—"

"Fine for the moment." He nodded toward the house, not willing to discuss his mother right now. "You've got a party to get to."

"Yes. Yes." She glanced at him and then away again. "Tell her hello. Will you?"

"I will." And he would. His mother would be touched. She had always liked Kate and would give him a hard time, as she had before, for not pursuing *that Rainbolt girl* a little harder. As if trying harder was all it took to change things.

He followed Kate as she stepped into the now cozy living area of the small home and waved a hand around the room toward a buffet table, where folks he recognized had already lined up.

"Help yourself. Luna brought more food than I've ever seen. I'll be in leftover heaven for weeks."

No one in Rebel with any sense bypassed

anything the ranch chef prepared, and that included him. He filled his plate and settled in a chair across the room near the open French doors, where guests had spilled out onto a cozy patio.

From his position, Jess could see everything, and he stayed there for almost an hour while he cleaned his plate and nursed a glass of sweet tea. All the Rainbolt brothers were here with their wives. Mitch, Reece and Tucker were attentive to their little sister and took care of the guests, not allowing Kate to do anything except enjoy the party in her honor. It was clear they were happy to have her back in the fold.

Despite their rocky past, he had to admit he was glad for Kate and her brothers. Jess had always envied the dynamics among the Rainbolts. His own mother had been close with Kate's mother once upon a time, before she'd fallen from grace and married TJ Rainbolt. Then their social circles hadn't crossed, and according to his mother, Jess's dad had discouraged the friendship the same way he'd discouraged Jess's relationship with Kate.

What his father had never understood was that, while the Rainbolts were poor in many things, they were rich when it came to love and their dedication to each other.

Kate's laughter rang out, and Jess turned to see her chatting with Finn Hardy, the vet who worked at the equine clinic housed at Rebel Ranch. When the cowboy bent his head close to her ear, Jess clenched his jaw.

"He's pretty smooth, ain't he?" Willard asked as he sidled up next to Jess and sat down in an empty chair. "We both could learn something from his technique."

"Who?" Jess feigned interest in the bottom of his glass.

"That vet feller."

"Can't fault Finn. He's a nice guy."

"Sure he is, but you know that means you're gonna have to move faster if you want to catch Miss Kate's eye."

Jess jerked his head around to be sure he'd heard Willard correctly. "What are you jabbering about?"

"You heard me. Don't be staring at me like I'm a steer with two heads."

"I'm not here to catch anyone's eye," Jess shot back. If only his life were that simple. He was in Rebel because his mother's kidney disease had worsened, and she had begun dialysis while she waited for a transplant. When he wasn't working at the ranch, he and his sister took turns driving his mother to her dialysis appointments in Tulsa three times a week. There was no time for anything else.

"No?" Willard continued. "Looks like you have anyhow."

"Now what are you talking about?"

"That cowgirl by the dessert table is eyeing you. I do believe she works in the kitchen with Chef Luna. Sure would be nice to end up with a woman who can cook, right?"

Jess nearly laughed aloud. There was a time when he believed that he'd end up with Kate. A woman who ten years ago couldn't boil water. He couldn't help but wonder if that had changed.

"What are you smirking for?" Willard asked.

"Me? Nothing," Jess said. He nodded toward the cowgirl. "She's checking out the lemon meringue pie from Daisy Rainbolt's bakery. Sure hope there's more than one, or hearts are going to break tonight. Mitch's wife makes the best pies around. Don't you think?"

Willard jumped from his seat. "I do, and lemon meringue is my favorite." The old cowboy gave a thumbs-up. "I'll catch you later."

Jess chuckled and stood to take a stroll around the living room, hoping that Willard wouldn't follow.

He scanned the space. The home had been empty last time he was here. Now the little ranch house had personality. Kate's. He stopped to check out a painting next to a display shelf. The Southwest colors did indeed remind him of his sister's pottery.

"Like it?"

He turned to find Kate behind him. "Yeah, I do."

"It's from San Antonio. A little shop on the River Walk."

"You get around, don't you?"

She smiled at his words. He hadn't purposely complimented her. It was an observation. One she was proud of, he realized when her face lit up.

"I've been to nearly every state west of the Mississippi in the last ten years."

"I'm not surprised." What surprised him was that she was in Rebel, acting like she might settle down.

Jess reached out a hand to straighten the picture frame, but it refused to cooperate. He peeked at the wall behind the frame, confused.

"As it turns out, it's impossible to hang a picture with one arm," Kate said.

"I'm not following."

"I tried to hold the nail with my casted arm, but it hurt to raise it that high. So I swung at the wall really quick and made a few dents in the plaster. The picture is hanging there to cover up the holes in the wall. It won't ever hang straight."

"A little spackle will fix that right up." His gaze moved to the walnut bookshelf and a framed photo in black-and-white. "This your family?"

"Yes. When we were kids." She pointed to each face. "Mitch. Reece. Tucker. That's me, next to Levi."

"I'm sorry about Levi." His mother had told him the Rainbolts had lost their youngest sibling six years ago. "I never said that, and I meant to."

"Thanks."

Jess couldn't help but look at the rest of the items on display. Everything on the shelves was a piece of the puzzle that made up Kate's life. They were the steps that had brought her back to Rebel. Long ago, she had confided to him that she'd planned to find her father. Had she? Or was she still on that journey, temporarily sidelined by the accident in Tucson?

He nodded to the collection of miniature glass horses. "What's this?"

"Oh, it's silly, I guess. My father started my obsession with the figurines. He brought me back one or two when he was on the circuit. I started picking one up at each stop on the road. They've been in storage until now."

"They're beautiful."

"Handblown, fused glass, they tell me. I've broken a few along the way. They cut and leave you bleeding mercilessly if you break them."

"I guess anything beautiful comes with risks." He pointed to an amber glass stallion with a blue mane. "Why does that look familiar?"

Kate picked up the figurine. "I showed this to you a long time ago. It's the last one my father brought me. I was eight. It's been in storage for a long time." She raised a shoulder. "I've never thought of myself as a collector. I pulled the figurines out of a packing box this week and realized how many I've accumulated. I probably should get rid of them."

"No. Don't."

Kate's gaze met his, her eyes reflecting surprise. "That sounds like you have a definite opinion on the subject."

He hadn't thought much about it until this moment. "Collections are a way to preserve the past. Someday you'll have children to pass them on to."

"You must have spotted those flying pigs at the ranch," she said.

Jess laughed at the reference. "You're good at poking fun at yourself, aren't you?"

"Am I?"

"Yeah."

"What do you collect?" Kate asked.

Jess pondered the question for a moment. Maybe he collected memories. Memories that he unfolded at night and examined because he was still trying to understand his own path.

"That wasn't supposed to be a hard question," she said.

"Let me think about it," he returned.

Someone called her name, and she waved across the room. "If you'll excuse me."

Jess watched her float away, and then his gaze returned to the glass horses with their sharp edges. Just like Kate. Delicate and beautiful and poised to gallop away at any moment, and he'd be left bleeding if he got too close.

"Is this an intervention?" Kate asked. She stared at all three of her brothers across her kitchen table. Mitch, Reece and even Tucker had appeared on her doorstep after church. They stared at her with earnest expressions, and she eyed them suspiciously in return.

Sure, they'd brought Eagle donuts, but her gut still told her something was about to go down, and it wasn't good.

"This is a show of support and concern," Mitch said.

She picked up her coffee mug and took it to the sink to rinse.

"Kate?" Tucker asked softly. "Did you see Dr. Bowie at the clinic this week?"

"Yes, and only because you all ganged up on me."

"Come on. You had to have your arm evaluated eventually. We only nudged you along," Tucker returned.

"Okay, great. My arm is healing nicely."

Healing nicely, but the doc had concerns about her concussion and had referred her to a neurologist in Tulsa. Information her brothers didn't need to know.

Kate dried her hand and turned to face them, smiling sweetly. It was time to take control of the situation. "Did you know Dr. Bowie used to barrel race?"

"Oh, yeah?" Reece asked. "When was that?"

Mitch turned to him. "Focus. We're here for a reason."

"Right. Right."

Here for a reason. The truth was about to land.

Tucker waved Kate to the chair. "Sit down, would you?"

Tucker of all people, was in on this ambush. He was the closest to her in age. Only three years separated them. They were the youngest siblings. Weren't they supposed to stick together?

She slid back onto the chair and sighed.

"I couldn't help but notice a few things at your party on Saturday," Tucker said.

Her head jerked up. "What things?"

"You grimace when you laugh, and you hold your middle. A few times, you seemed to have difficulty catching your breath. That tells me that, at minimum, you've injured a few ribs and you're in more than a little pain."

Leave it to the eagle-eyed vet. Now she'd have to talk her way around that observation.

She smiled at Tucker. "Is that all? Everyone who mounts a horse gets a cracked rib or two."

"Cracked ribs and maybe a concussion? Most bullfighters don't wear helmets, do they?"

She swallowed hard and ran a finger over the lid of the blue-and-white Eagle Donuts box.

When she didn't answer, Tucker continued. "Doesn't matter. Helmets don't necessarily keep you from a concussion." He cocked his head in thought. "I'd like some details on your accident. I'm guessing there's more going on than you've told us."

Kate's hand moved to her neckline, and she fingered the edges of her collar to be sure the fabric covered her scar. "Why are you asking me all these questions?"

"Mitch told you. Because we're concerned." Tucker reached out to take her hand. "And we've come to the conclusion that you cannot do physical labor on the ranch for a while. It's too risky. You have to heal."

"So, none of you believe I'm qualified to handle the horses?"

"This isn't about the horses," Reece said. "Kate, you're qualified to do any job you want on this ranch. We'd like more than anything for you to learn the workings of the entire ranch and become a full-fledged partner. Trouble is, you're not in any shape for that right now."

Kate scanned the table, looking at her brothers one by one. They didn't flinch. "What are you saying?"

"We don't want to see you near the horses," Reece said, his voice firm. "It's too dangerous."

"You're grounding me? Like I'm sixteen again?" She bit her lip, stunned at what she was hearing.

"How long did the doctor tell you it would take until she can give you a health release?" Tucker asked.

She eyed him slowly. Usually, Tucker was the voice of reason against her big brothers, but she could tell he wasn't going to budge either. This wasn't good. Kate turned her head. "I refuse to answer on the grounds that it will give you more ammunition."

"Fine. Then you are grounded," Reece said. He took a casual sip of coffee from the mug in front of him.

"This is ridiculous. I've been hurt plenty of times. I get back in the saddle. No one has ever told me I can't ride or do my job."

"We are now." Reece's jaw was set as he met her gaze. "Because this is our rodeo."

She was between a rock and a hard place. She was going to be jobless for six weeks and had mounting medical bills, and if she left Rebel Ranch, she'd also need to board

Einstein. Here, she had rent-free housing, but she needed a paycheck.

"Kate," Tucker added. "This situation has left you feeling out of control. We get that. We're Rainbolts. All of our lives have been a series of out-of-control events. From losing Mom to Dad walking out to Levi's death." He paused long enough to make her turn and look at him. Tucker had been through the worst of the worst, losing his children's mother soon after their birth.

His eyes were glassy with moisture as he stared at her. "We can't lose you, Kate."

Choked up, she nodded.

"Your health is the most important thing," Tucker continued.

"You'll be back in the saddle before you know it," Reece said.

Mitch leaned forward, his blue eyes boring into hers. "We're so proud of what you've accomplished, Bug. You need to know that we're behind you one hundred percent. Even when money was tight, we always made sure there was enough for your horse and boarding and anything else our girl needed."

Mitch was right, and she was ashamed of herself for pushing back.

"I'm sorry. I know that." She swallowed. "It's just that I'm not used to sitting around, and I have bills…"

"We'll pay your bills," Tucker said.

"No. Absolutely not." She paid her own way. That was rule number one.

Reece leaned back in the chair and nodded thoughtfully. "There's a solution here, if you're willing to consider it."

"What kind of solution?"

"If you can commit to sticking around to help launch the tourist season, I'll offer you a chance to use your degree."

"My degree? I graduated ten years ago." She wasn't sure if she even remembered half the classes she'd taken in college.

"I've been managing the ranch books," Reece said. "That's all I'm asking you to do. We outsource payroll and have an accountant for the tax stuff."

"A desk job." Kate groaned.

"It's not the end of the world," Mitch said.

"I need help," Reese explained. "By all indications, you need a job."

"A desk job."

"A desk job. You'll handle the books for all aspects of the guest ranch, liaise with the accountant for the ranch."

"What do you mean, all aspects?"

"Anything that doesn't have to do with employees."

Once again, her gaze took in each of her brothers, trying to figure out how she'd ended up in this situation. No one knew the details of her injuries except Franny. Kate inhaled sharply. And Jess.

"What do you think, Kate?" Tucker asked.

"I think that I'm going to give Jess McNally a piece of my mind." She stood and headed toward the door.

"Kate, come back here," Mitch called.

"Jess didn't have anything to do with this," Reece yelled after her.

Kate blew a raspberry and kept walking until she got to the main stable and the office at the back. She shoved open the door without knocking.

Jess glanced over his shoulder and then swiveled his chair around, his eyes round.

"You told my brothers about the accident," she said.

"No." Jess shook his head slowly. "That's not what happened. Reece asked me a question, and I answered. I told you I wouldn't lie."

"What question was that?"

"He asked if I thought you were ready to work in the stables. I said no."

"Thanks a lot," she sputtered with a shake of her head. "From this point on, you'd better steer clear of me, McNally."

Jess shrugged, nonplussed. "I understand that you may be handling the books for the ranch going forward, and that will include talking to me."

"If I do, that doesn't mean I have to acknowledge your existence."

"How's it going to work when you're released by the doctor and I'm your boss?"

"I don't know, but I'm still a Rainbolt,

and this is still my family's ranch, so unless you can find a way to get rid of me, I'm not going away."

"No one wants to get rid of you, Kate. As far as I can tell, everyone is bending over backward to keep you in Rebel."

Kate refused to look him in the eye. A part of her realized that she was being irrational, and yet her pride wouldn't allow her to admit that. For ten years, she'd managed her life and her destiny. The world she'd built had come crashing down because of a single night in the arena and less than two weeks back in Rebel.

Jess McNally was the catalyst here. The man had betrayed her, proving that he'd held a grudge because she'd turned down his proposal. He'd thrown her under the bus the first chance he'd gotten.

Turning on her heel, she left his office, not even stopping to greet Einstein as she passed the stalls.

Pull it together, she told herself as her boots echoed on the stable floor. She'd hit rock bottom before, except this time, she didn't have anything but her horse left. Yes, she had a job at Rebel Ranch, but going from rodeo girl to office girl was a bitter pill to swallow.

Oh, she'd do it, all right. She'd heal her body and prove to everyone that she wasn't broken. By then, maybe she'd know whether or not she was going to be able to stay in Rebel or if she should move on.

Chapter Four

Kate's phone buzzed, and she glanced at the screen as she stood in line at the Rebel bank.

The neurologist. It was Friday, and the specialist's office had left two messages since Monday in an attempt to schedule her appointment in Tulsa, thanks to Dr. Bowie's referral.

Another doctor. Another session of being poked and prodded and then billed was more than Kate could deal with or afford right now. Besides, she wasn't sure she even needed to see a neurologist. The CT she'd had done in Tucson had revealed a hairline fracture that would heal on its own. She hadn't had a dizzy spell since the unfortunate incident in the barn with Jess watching a week ago. Why go looking for trouble when it so often found her anyhow?

She'd made a pact with her brothers and committed to sticking around until the summer tourist season launched after Memorial Day, and then they'd discuss her options. She'd take on the equine position full time or hit the road. If her arm continued to heal as anticipated, the cast might even be off before the hoedown, and then she'd take a little time to evaluate the whole work-for-Jess situation before she made any decisions.

Right now, having choices was absolutely her top priority. That would be her focus when she found herself claustrophobically running numbers in a windowless room.

After completing the transaction for the ranch, Kate shoved the deposit slip into her back pocket and left. She stood on the sidewalk outside the bank, eyeing Main Street. The town certainly had evolved. When she was growing up, Rebel had looked like every other dusty small town. Now it had personality.

Kate smiled at the quaint scene before her. Flowers hung from giant pots on the street corners, and wrought iron benches had been placed at intervals along the long sidewalks. Charming shops with clever window decorations and chalk sidewalk signs beckoned.

Most of the businesses had navy canvas awnings, including her sister-in-law Daisy's bakery on the corner. Kate's gaze skimmed the shops on the other side of Main Street. Tallgrass Inn was directly across from the bank. To the right was Rebel Reads. A small shop was tucked between the bookstore and the diner. The Saucy Potter. Kate chuckled. That had to be Nicole's pottery store.

A quick check of her phone confirmed it was nearly noon. She had an hour for lunch, which was what Violet and the other employees in the admin building took. She wouldn't abuse the rules because she was Reece's sister. Satisfied there was plenty of time to peek into the shop and then stop by Tucker's vet clinic, she proceeded to the crosswalk at Main and First.

Resisting the urge to jaywalk, Kate stood at the corner, tapping her boot toe on the concrete as she waited for the light to change. Rebel boasted one traffic signal, and it had the onerous reputation of taking its good old time, without particular attention to the number of cars lined up on Main or First. Currently, Main Street was bumper-to-bumper with one pickup and a tractor. Another busy day in Rebel.

On green, she dashed across the intersection to the other side of the street. The artfully decorated storefront window of the Saucy Potter held a large coral-colored pitcher overflowing with branches of pussy willow. Matching mugs hung from the ceiling at different levels, and stacks of dinnerware were creatively displayed in the forefront of the window, resting on swaths of crinkled muslin fabric. A small wooden stepstool held other matching pieces of the same color design on each step. The entire display urged passersby to stop and look.

Kate smiled and reached for the handle on the shop's glossy burgundy front door. A small chime sounded as she pulled it open and stepped into the brightly lit store. The scent of something that she couldn't put her finger on wrapped itself around her.

"Welcome. Be right there." The voice called from somewhere in the depths of the space, and a moment later, Jess's older sister, Nicole, appeared.

"Kate! How nice to see you." Dark-haired and petite, Nicole pulled a canvas smock from around her neck and tossed it on the glass counter. She offered Kate a light hug and glanced at her arm. "Jess wasn't kidding. You really were run over, weren't you?"

"I'm fine. In one piece and healing nicely." She smiled. "I wanted to thank you for the mugs. I love them."

"You're so welcome." Nicole peeked at her phone.

"And I love your shop." Kate waved her

free hand. "When I left town, you were about to start med school. This is quite a departure."

The other woman groaned. "Oh, yes. Medical school. I didn't have the guts to flat out tell my father no, so I did the next best thing. I eloped." She grimaced and looked around. "I hope we're alone. That sounded awfully flippant."

"No, it didn't. I completely get it." And Kate did. Dr. McNally had been a well-meaning authoritarian. It had always been his way or the highway. Period.

Nicole sighed and shook her head. "My father was a wonderful man, but he didn't understand my dreams... Jess's either. I suppose because they weren't his dreams. Anyhow, now I'm a single mother of a nine-year-old, and I'm happily running my own life." She reached for a business card and handed it to Kate. "I'm online too. We sell pottery all over the country."

"That's wonderful." Kate examined a display of bowls that matched her mug.

"This place might be very dangerous to my budget."

Nicole laughed. "That's what I'm hoping."

"It smells nice in here," Kate observed.

"Ha! A little trick. I have lemon, fresh rosemary and vanilla simmering on a hot plate in the back. It makes the place smell like those expensive specialty shops in the city."

"It's working. I find it very appealing. I'll keep it in mind the next time I set the oven on fire."

"You're kidding, right?"

"If only I was."

Once again, Nicole peeked at her phone.

"Is everything okay?" Kate asked.

"I'm sorry. My mom was supposed to be here a few minutes ago so I can pick up my daughter, Olive, from school. The elementary school is letting out early for teacher training."

As if on cue, the front door burst open, the chimes dancing with a noisy refrain. "I'm here. Sorry to be late."

"Mom. Where were you? You didn't answer my text."

"Sorry. Lunch with the church ladies." Susan McNally tossed the ends of her purple-fringed scarf over her shoulder. When she saw Kate, her eyes widened with clear delight.

"Kate! I would have left the last bite of dessert if I'd known you were here." Jess's mother reached for Kate's hand.

"Mrs. McNally. How nice to see you." Jess's mother was as lovely as ever, though Kate couldn't help but notice she'd lost a bit of weight and seemed almost frail.

"Now, now. Call me Susan. You're not a schoolgirl anymore." She smiled. "And look at you with that pretty dark hair dipped in purple. It's my favorite color."

"Is it? Mine, as well."

"How are you?" Susan glanced at Kate's cast. "Jess mentioned your accident."

"He's a little like *The Weekly Rebel*, isn't he?" Kate observed, referring to the town newspaper. "All the news that's fit to be told."

Susan laughed. "Men like to call women verbal information systems, but I disagree. They do their fair share of chatting."

Kate smiled at the comment.

"Exactly," Nicole said. She reached behind the counter and pulled out a purse. "I'm sorry to leave, Kate, but elementary school waits for no one and Olive worries if I'm late."

"Good to see you," Kate said. She turned back to Susan. "I stopped in to thank Nicole for the housewarming present that Jess brought over."

"Oh, the firebrand mugs." Susan nodded. "Those are my favorite. We have matching plates too."

"I'll have to put those on my wish list." Kate grimaced as a sharp pain shot through her arm.

"Are you okay?"

"Yes. Sometimes the cast pinches."

Susan stepped forward and gently examined Kate's arm. "I imagine so. The arm will swell and pinch in that plaster if you aren't diligent about elevating it."

When Kate looked at her with surprise, Susan chuckled. "Don't mind me. Once a nurse, always a nurse. I'm sure you've been told enough times to elevate the arm."

"I have, but I should do it more, so your advice is a good reminder." Kate smiled. "I never knew you were a nurse."

"Oh, I retired when Nicky was born," Susan said. "Did you know that your momma almost went to nursing school too?"

"My mother? No."

"Yes." Susan nodded. "Both of us were accepted into a three-year program. Margaret changed her mind once she fell in love with TJ Rainbolt." She shrugged. "Then the babies came along. It took me a while to catch up with her. Nicky is the same age as Tucker. Your momma got a head start with Mitch and Reece."

Kate nodded, savoring the details about her mother as she did the math. Her mother had given birth to Mitch and Reece when she could have been in college. Then along came Tucker. Fourteen years after

Mitch, Kate had been born and then Levi. The Rainbolt matriarch had passed away twenty-two years ago. She'd been the same age Mitch was today. Kate blinked. The train of thought left her reeling.

"Are you all right?" Susan asked.

"Yes. I guess I never realized that my mother had three kids by the time she was thirty and then two more later on. Here I am, nearly thirty-one, and I can't even imagine how she managed everything."

"The good Lord doesn't give us more than we can handle. But you're right. Your momma had her hands full, and most of the time, she juggled it alone."

"How did she afford five kids?"

"Margaret was whip-smart, especially when it came to numbers. She did book-keeping for a few of the local businesses, and she cleaned houses. Took you and Levi with her."

"Yes. I remember that." Kate looked at Susan. "How did you know? I thought you lost touch."

Susan sighed. "We did keep up. I'm

sorry to say I was a coward in those days. I wouldn't defy my husband, who didn't understand my relationship with your mother. Though every now and again, when Jacob was out of town for some medical conference, your mother and I managed to get together." Her eyes became glassy with unshed tears. "I'm ashamed of myself. What kind of friend was I?"

"I'm sure my mother understood," Kate said.

"I hope so." She offered a weak smile. "That reminds me. I've been sorting through things. Downsizing. I found pictures of your momma from high school." She looked at Kate. "Why don't you stop by the house after church? Join us for lunch, and I'll give them to you."

"I've been invited to my brother Mitch's for lunch."

"Then how about dessert? I'd love nothing more than time to chat with you. About three o'clock?"

"All right. I'd like that." Kate paused.

"Susan, Jess mentioned you've been a little under the weather."

The older woman raised her brows. "Jess feels the need to protect me. I'm fighting a battle with my body, and some days are more difficult than others."

"Pardon me?"

"Kidneys. I've struggled with kidney disease all my life."

"I'm so sorry."

"It is what it is." She shrugged, dismissing the topic. "So I'll see you on Sunday afternoon?"

"Yes, ma'am."

Behind them, the door opened and Jess strode in, his eyes on his phone. He raised his head and stopped the moment he saw her.

"Kate," he said. His face remained without expression, though his eyes locked on her as though she were trespassing.

Kate started to speak but found herself tongue-tied, her thoughts jumbled by Jess's unexpected appearance. She'd managed to avoid him for nearly an entire week, and now she didn't even know what to say. She cleared her throat. "I better get going. I'm on my lunch break, and I promised my brother Tucker that I'd stop by his clinic."

She gave Jess a curt nod as she headed out the door. Now she regretted agreeing to dessert with Susan. What if Jess showed up?

After driving around the block, she parked in front of Rebel Vet and Rescue and walked in through one of the entry doors.

"Miss Kate!" Magnolia "Nolie" Parker, the receptionist, popped up from her desk and came around to greet her. "I heard you were back." She shook her head and clucked her tongue. "What did you do to yourself?"

"Tucker didn't tell you?"

"Please. Your brother is so closemouthed, he's useless when it comes to gossip... I mean, news."

Kate gave an abridged version of her accident, though she was tempted to pull a Willard Cornell and come up with a tall tale.

Nolie once again clucked her tongue. "I'll have Dr. Rainbolt run a little of my special chicken noodle soup over to you tomorrow. It cures everything from gout to the common cold."

"That's so sweet of you," Kate said. She assessed the busy, divided waiting room. One side was for dogs and the other for cats. "Is my brother around?"

"He's in the back room with a new customer." She grinned. "Now I know why."

"What's that mean?"

"Oh, you'll find out soon enough."

Kate peeked over the desk where a familiar canine lay stretched on her back, half in and half out of a dog bed, snoring softly. "Ernie!" She well remembered the dog who'd been in the wedding party at Tucker and Jena's wedding in December.

"Yes. Ernie's in charge around here."

Kate and Nolie turned when the dog-entrance door opened and Saylor Tuttle, the pastor's wife, walked in with an English bulldog on a pink leash.

As Mrs. Tuttle opened her mouth to

greet Kate, Nolie grabbed Kate's hand and yanked her around the reception desk urgently.

"Be right with you, Mrs. Tuttle." She looked at Kate. "You come with me."

"Where are we going?" Kate asked as they moved down the hall.

"Your brother's office. If I leave you out there, Mrs. Tuttle will want to pick your brain, and it won't be pleasant."

"Did they remodel back here?" Kate asked as she followed the receptionist.

"Yes. Dr. Harper... I mean, Dr. Rainbolt got a new office, and they added a playroom." Nolie shook her head. "I can't tell you how confusing it is now that they both have the same last name." She knocked on a door and stepped in with Kate in tow. "Dr. Rainbolt, your sister is here."

Tucker sat behind a huge desk wearing a white lab coat, with a stethoscope around his neck. It didn't matter how long he'd been a vet, Kate still got a kick out of seeing him in a lab coat. He'd come a long way from the trailer park.

"Thanks, Nolie," he said.

Kate turned to the receptionist, as well. "Yes, thank you."

"My pleasure."

As Nolie left, Tucker came around the desk and placed a kiss on her forehead. "You're right on time. Jena wanted to be here, but she got called away to see a patient." He looked her up and down. "You look good. How are you feeling?"

"Better. Much better. I like your house. My insomnia has disappeared since I moved in."

"Glad to hear that."

Kate glanced around. "Nolie said you were with a new customer?"

"That's right. I've got a friend to introduce you to."

"Tucker, I don't do blind dates. You know that."

"This is a different blind date." He led her down the hall to a room filled with bins of animal toys, a few bean bag chairs and several cat towers. A lean gray-and-white cat sat at the window ledge, its focus on a bird feeder that hung from a large maple tree outside.

"Your friend is a cat?"

"That's right."

"Tucker." Kate sighed. Over the years, her brother had worked hard to get her to adopt an animal. She'd always held him at bay with the excuse that she'd be back on the road again in a day or two.

Kate stood in the doorway, slowly shaking her head. "Tuck, I can't take on a cat. I don't know if I'm staying in Rebel."

"We can deal with that if you actually leave."

"I don't know how to care for a cat," she continued.

"Cats are self-sufficient and independent. This cat more than most."

"You say that like it's a bad thing."

Tucker smiled. "Like you, Bella has attitude."

"Now you're insulting me."

"No, I'm not. Though there are a few more similarities, which is why I thought of you when Bella needed a home."

"Such as?"

"She's always getting into trouble, and she's a one-human cat. Very much a loner. Bella doesn't play well with others."

"Hey, that's not nice. I play well with others."

"But you prefer to be alone."

"There is nothing wrong with being a loner." Kate walked up to the window ledge and held out a hand to the animal. "Right, Bella?"

Bella sniffed and gazed at Kate with wide, forlorn green eyes. Then, as if approving, she bumped her head into Kate's hand.

"That's the universal sign you may pet her," Tucker said. "Stick to the top of the head until she gets to know you."

"Gets to know me? Tucker, I can barely remember to water my plants. I'm not ready for a pet."

"If you forget to feed her, she will let you know. No worries."

The door creaked open, and Nolie peeked

her head in and looked from Tucker to Kate. "Do we have a match?"

"I'm not sure," Kate said.

"This sweet darling was surrendered because the owner's boyfriend had allergies. Imagine that," Nolie said with a cluck of her tongue.

"That's terrible," Kate murmured. When Bella met her gaze, the green eyes searching, almost expectant, Kate's resolve began to melt.

"Right? I'd have gotten rid of the boyfriend first," Nolie said.

"Me too." Kate frowned. "Why isn't Bella next door at the rescue?"

"No room at the inn," Tucker said. "We'll have an adoption event Memorial Weekend, but right now, we're at full capacity. Even the foster homes are full. It's always that way during kitten season."

"I don't know..." Kate murmured. This was a huge responsibility, and she definitely was not the maternal type. Besides, horses were the only animals she knew anything about.

"How about if you foster Bella?" Tucker asked. "If it doesn't work out, for whatever reason, I'll make other arrangements."

Kate released a resigned breath. "Okay, I guess I can do that. It is a big house for one diva. We should be able to respect each other's personal space."

When Tucker looked at Nolie, and they both grinned, Kate was certain she'd been had.

Bella began to virtuously lick her paws and groom herself as though she understood she was the topic of discussion.

The docile feline changed her tune when she went into the carrier. She began to wail at full volume once Tucker fastened the seat belt around her carrier in the back seat of Kate's truck.

"This is perfectly normal," Tucker assured her.

"Perfectly normal?" Kate muttered. A mile outside Rebel, she turned on the radio to a country-western oldies station. Bella paused mid wail when Toby Keith hit a low note.

"Well, what do you know? You like music." Kate jacked up the sound, which prompted the feline to settle in the carrier and fall asleep.

When Kate pulled into the ranch's gravel drive, Mitch stepped out of the admin building and waved her over.

Kate slowed the truck to a stop and rolled down her window.

"You have a hearing problem?" Mitch asked.

"Oh, sorry." She turned off the radio.

"That's better. So how's the desk jockey's first week?"

She rolled her eyes. "I just made a bank deposit. Doesn't get much more thrilling than that."

"Hang in there, Bug. You'll be looking at this episode of your life in your rearview mirror before you know it."

"Not soon enough," she muttered. "Mitch, did you know that momma and Susan McNally were friends?"

"Sure."

"And that they stayed friends after they were married?"

He shook his head and offered a musing smile. "Yeah, every now and again, Mrs. McNally came by for a visit. When Momma was sick, she had groceries sent over regularly, though she didn't want anyone to know it was her."

"How did you find out?"

"I went to town and weaseled the information out of Mrs. Leonard. She ran the Piggly Wiggly in those days."

Kate mulled the information for a moment. "That was nice of her."

"More than nice." He cocked his head as if remembering. "Thanks to her generosity, and a few others, we never went hungry."

"She invited me to dessert on Sunday. Will Daisy mind if I duck out of dinner early?"

"Oh, I forgot to tell you." He grimaced.

"Tell me what?"

"We have an outbreak of the nasties at the house. Dinner is canceled."

"What are the nasties?" Kate inched

away from the car door. "And are you contagious?"

"It's a stomach virus, and thanks to good hand washing, I do not have anything that might be contagious, just suffering from a lack of sleep."

"Oh, good."

He raised a brow. "Thanks a lot."

"You know what I mean."

Kate heard a car's engine and swiveled around in her seat. Jess's truck pulled into the parking area, the tires crunching on the gravel.

"I better get going. I have to drop off… um, a few things at the house before I get back to work."

Mitch chuckled and glanced back at Jess's truck. "So, Bug. How are you and Jess getting along?"

"Fine."

"Does that mean you're avoiding him?"

"Perhaps."

"Look, you're blaming the guy for something he didn't do."

Annoyance rattled right through Kate at

her brother's words, threatening to release her temper. She took a calming breath. "I know exactly what he did, Mitch. He had a chance to toss me a bone, and instead, he hung me out to dry."

"He told the truth. You can't blame a guy for that."

"Sure I can. Absolutely I can. And do." She fumed for a moment at the thought of how Jess had double-crossed her. The man had changed. Years ago, she could count on him when her back was against the wall. Not anymore.

Mitch smiled, obviously seeing humor in the situation that she did not. "I'm fighting a losing battle here, aren't I?"

"Sure are." Kate looked at him. "You waved me down. Did you have something to tell me?"

"I did. We outsource HR here, and Violet said your packet with an employee handbook and payroll paperwork hasn't arrived yet. I wanted to be sure you knew about staff meetings. They're held every Monday morning in the conference room at 7:00 a.m., unless Reece is out of town."

"I'll be there, representing the pencil pushers of Rebel Ranch."

"Do you hate your job? Really?" He tipped back his Stetson and narrowed his eyes, assessing her.

Kate raised a shoulder. "It's not so bad."

After a week, she'd nailed the bookkeeping part of her job. Her innate talent for numbers had returned, and the job had become almost fun. Now she could spend less time in the chair and a little more figuring out ranch operations live. But her brother didn't need to know that.

Mitch held up a hand. "Did you hear that sound?"

"Nope. Didn't hear a thing."

"Kate. That was a cat." Mitch started laughing as he moved to peer in the cab seat of the truck. "That's a carrier. You have a cat in there."

"Okay, yes," she admitted. "There is a cat in the back seat. What of it?"

"Not a thing." Mitch grinned and crossed his arms.

"Have you ever gone up against Tucker at his clinic?"

"I sure have." He gave a slow nod. "You agreed to fostering, right?"

Kate's jaw sagged at his words. "How did you know that?"

"Ask me about my foster animals sometime."

A door slammed shut, and Kate quickly checked the reflection in the truck's side-view mirror. Uh-oh, Jess was headed her way. She nodded to Mitch. "Gotta run."

He chuckled and stepped back from the truck.

This wasn't a laughing matter. She had managed to avoid Jess all week, and she'd like to continue the pattern.

Once home, she put the supplies from the clinic on the counter. She released Bella from her carrier and followed the animal as she sniffed her way through the house. Tucker had kept cats and a dog in here. No doubt she smelled the animals.

When Bella jumped on the window ledge in the living room, Kate put her blanket and toys from the clinic on the floor. Tucker said it was important for Bella to have familiar scents. He knew what he was doing.

Kate did not. She was a horse person. Definitely not a cat person. What could she do with a cat? As she put out bowls of water and dry food, she shook her head. This was a mistake.

She thought about the long-limbed cowboy with the dark eyes who had broken her confidence. Yes, this was one in a long line of mistakes of late.

"This a very bad idea," Jess muttered. He pulled his truck into his mother's drive and stared at Kate's beater of a pickup at the curb next to his sister's little compact car. His mother hadn't mentioned Kate when he said he'd stop by today. For a moment, he toyed with the idea of going right back where he'd come from. But he'd promised himself he wouldn't let his mother down again, and he intended to keep his word.

Grabbing flowers from the seat, Jess strode to the front door and knocked on the screen frame before he let himself in. "Hey, Mom."

"We're in the kitchen, Jess," his mother called out.

Jess stepped into the kitchen, where Nicole and Olive sat at the table while his mother arranged a bouquet of gerbera daisies in a vase. He glanced down at the pink carnations in his hand.

"You brought flowers too," his mother said. "Don't I feel spoiled?"

"Except Nicky upstaged me with the fancy daisies." He stared at his sister.

Nicole put her coffee mug down and shook her head. "It wasn't me, little brother."

"It was me."

He swung around to find Kate in the doorway. Her face was without expression, but her eyes...oh, those eyes. They laughed at him.

"I invited Kate for dessert," his mother said. "Isn't it nice that she could join us?"

Nice. Real nice.

"Do you want some stew?" his mother asked him.

"You said dessert."

"I did, but it's been hours since lunch, hasn't it? I tried a new recipe from one of my church friends." She gestured with a hand. "Sit down, both of you."

Outnumbered, he sat at the table. When he inched his chair away from Kate's, his sister silently laughed at him from across the table.

He turned to the stove in time to see his mother ladling a generous amount of stew into a bowl. "Just a little, Mom," he said.

Ignoring his request, she placed a large bowlful in front of him along with half a loaf of fresh bread.

Jess scratched his head. Okay. So he'd take the rest home for dinner for the next two nights.

Kate eyed her own bowl and smiled before digging in.

"How's it taste?" his mother asked a few minutes later.

"Mom, you know you're the best cook in Rebel," Jess said. That was the absolute truth, and the savory stew was no exception.

"It pains me to agree with my dear brother," Nicole said. "But he's right."

"This is amazing, Susan," Kate chimed in.

"I'll give you the recipe."

"I, um…" Kate's face pinked. "Thank you."

When she kept her eyes downward, clearly not wanting to meet his gaze, Jess bit back a grin. Kate's reputation as a terrible cook was apparently still intact.

A phone began to ring, and his mother paused. "Oh, I left my cell in my purse. I'll be right back."

"Take the recipe. She'll never know," Jess said once his mother left the room.

"Very funny." Kate scooped another mouthful without looking at him.

Nicole glanced back and forth between them. "What am I missing here?"

"Kate doesn't cook," he said.

Nicole's eyes widened. "Where are your manners, Jess? You haven't seen her in how many years? People change."

"No," Kate said with a shrug. "He's right. I can't cook. I was born without the culinary gene. I've gone from bad to pathetic with time." She stared at Jess. "Although I resent the fact that you didn't even give me the benefit of the doubt."

"Your face told the story," Jess said. "You turned red."

Olive giggled and wiped her mouth with a napkin.

"Can you cook, Olive?" Kate asked.

"Uh-huh. My mom and I are making a cookbook together."

"That's so nice." Kate released a sigh and studied his mother's old-fashioned floral cotton tablecloth. "My big brother, Mitch, tried to make sure everyone could cook. His specialty is mac and cheese. Reece's is meat loaf and sweet potato casserole.

Tucker is the omelet guy." She offered a sad, wistful smile. "Even my little brother, Levi, cooked. Grilled cheese and this amazing tomato soup from scratch."

"Do you have a specialty?" Olive asked.

"Cereal and milk." Carefully placing the spoon in the empty bowl, Kate carried both to the sink. "Mitch tried with me and gave up. He said it was safer that way and that I had other talents."

Jess hid a smile behind his hand. It was hard to stay annoyed at Kate. She so readily laughed at herself. Sure, she had a chip on her shoulder and refused to look reality square in the eye at times, but she was a good person.

A small voice in his head whispered, *Exactly why you need to stay far from the woman.*

"Miss Kate, I can give you cooking lessons," Olive said.

"Aw, Olive, that is so sweet of you," Kate said.

"I promised dessert." Jess's mother entered the room with a large cake on a glass stand. He stood, took it from her and placed it in the middle of the table.

"You made that?" Kate asked.

Susan smiled. "Not me. We were in Tulsa yesterday, and we stopped by Ludger's. I had it in the fridge in the garage for safe keeping."

"Ludger's?" Kate asked.

"Ludger's Bavarian Cakery. This is the red velvet Bavarian cream cheesecake," his mother said. "Red velvet cake on the top and bottom with vanilla and chocolate Bavarian cream swirled in the center."

Kate stared. "All that in one cake? That's amazing."

"Mom, are you supposed to have this?" Jess asked.

She eyed him with a lethal expression. "You watch your diet, and I'll watch mine. Fair enough?"

"Ouch," Jess muttered.

"My apologies to our guest," his mother continued. "My son thinks dialysis is a death sentence. Maybe it is. Maybe it's not, but I'm not going to live my life a prisoner to my body. A little cake isn't going to hurt. Moderation in everything is the key."

Kate's eyes widened, and he knew she was connecting the dots. "You were in Tulsa for dialysis," she said.

"Yes. Three times a week."

"If you ever need a backup driver, I'm free on Saturdays and Sundays," Kate said.

"That's so generous of you. I may take you up on that. Sometimes Nicky and Jess need a break."

"We don't need a break," Jess said.

"Speak for yourself," his sister said. "I think the appropriate answer here is thank you." She turned to Kate. "Thank you."

"Nicky, you cut the cake," his mother said. "I'm going to go get those photos that I promised Kate."

When his mother returned, she handed a large envelope to Kate. "You can look at these privately. If you have any questions, I can probably remember when and where they were taken."

"Thank you so much," Kate said. She accepted the envelope as though it was a precious bundle.

Margaret Rainbolt was the connection between Kate and his mother. Kate listened with rapt attention as his mother shared a few memories. His mother smiled and laughed like her old self as she talked. Jess found himself almost envious of the easy rapport between the two.

"Oh, I almost forgot," his mother said. She pulled a photo from her apron pocket and placed it on the table in front of Kate. "It's a Polaroid, so it's faded a bit."

"Is that you and my mother?" Kate asked.

"Yes. See that ribbon your mother is holding up? She won first place with her gingersnaps. I'll give you the recipe for that too, next time you're here."

"But Miss Kate can't cook," Olive said.

"Olive!" Nicole shushed her daughter.

"What?" Jess's mother looked from Olive to Kate.

Kate laughed. "My secret is out."

"You and I will make gingersnaps, Kate. That's a promise." A soft smile touched her lips as she looked at Kate. "You remind me so much of your momma, it just makes me happy inside."

Jess frowned at the words. Kate would no doubt be long gone before his mother could teach her anything, and this time, it would be his mother who would end up hurt. He couldn't, wouldn't let that happen.

When Kate stood to leave, Jess took that as a cue to depart too.

"Jess, take this box of leftovers to Kate's truck," his mother said. "I've got one for you, as well."

"Yeah, sure." He grabbed both boxes and followed Kate to her truck.

"Thank you," she murmured, avoiding eye contact.

Jess placed his box on the sidewalk before he slid hers onto the passenger seat of her truck. Stepping back, he searched for the right words. "Ah, Kate?"

She turned to him, her expression both wary and questioning.

"Don't take this the wrong way, but I

don't want my mother to get too attached to you."

Kate gasped, her blue eyes wide. "Excuse me?"

"She's a little needy right now. It's probably the prednisone."

"Are you telling me that I shouldn't be friends with your mother? Wow, the crab apple doesn't fall far from the tree. Like father, like son, right?"

"No. That's not it at all. I'm not my father, Kate." He paused and took a deep breath. "I just don't want her to get used to having you around and then have you disappear."

"You're overstepping here, Jess. Way overstepping." She looked him up and down and shook her head.

"I'm only being honest."

"Which you do so well. I believe the saying goes that sometimes discretion is the better part of valor. Maybe you should practice that instead, or think before you open your mouth to spout whatever unfiltered honesty you feel needs to be said."

He shoved his hands in his pocket. "Okay, my delivery needs work. Fair enough, but I'm only trying to protect my mother."

"I respect that, even if you are off base. You do realize that you're judging me based on our history, right?" She stared at him for a long moment, as if considering his words. "I suppose that's why you retaliated against me with my brothers."

"The fact that you dumped me never figured into the equation."

Kate glanced around as if hesitant to continue the discussion. She released a breath. "I did not dump you. I turned down your proposal."

"You dumped me."

"Look, let's be real. Your father didn't like me. He took issue with me being a Rainbolt. You and I would never have survived that obstacle." She sighed. "So let's move on, shall we? Call a truce?"

"I don't need a truce. We both work for Reece and Mitch. We're adults. End of story." He stared at her for a few moments. "You know, maybe you need to get over yourself. I didn't lie for you because it would've been the wrong thing to do."

Jess picked up his box and headed to his truck. He'd given Kate Rainbolt far more of his day off than he'd planned. He could guard his own heart, but now he'd have to protect his mother's, as well. The situation had just gotten complicated.

Chapter Five

~~

"Whoa, whoa, Mitch," Kate called out as her brother strode past her office.

He backed up and stepped inside the room, confusion on his face. "This is your office? I thought it was a supply closet."

"Same difference." She looked at him. "How are the kids? Recovering?"

"Yeah. Six cases of soda crackers and a dozen liters of lemon-lime sports drinks later." He rubbed his head. "It was a long weekend."

"I'm sorry."

"All part of being a parent. Your turn will come."

"Oh, I doubt that. I'm not mother material."

"Right." He chuckled and offered his usual knowing, brotherly look that she found annoying at times like this.

"How's Bella?" he asked.

"I don't want to talk about it."

"That well, huh?"

Kate didn't want to admit that Bella was growing on her. Cats were supposed to be aloof and distant. That's what Tucker had promised. He'd also warned her this particular cat was all that and a horse trailer full of attitude. He was wrong. The gray-and-white animal desperately longed for love and affection.

Bella hopped onto Kate's lap every chance she could and even snuggled next to her in bed at night. Bella had a routine too. She'd knead the comforter and then walk in a slow circle, finally curling up in a ball, her green eyes at half-mast until Kate turned off the light.

The situation had gotten so bad that Kate couldn't fall asleep unless Bella had settled in. How pathetic was that? She didn't need a cat. Or a reason to stay in Rebel. Now she had both.

Mitch glanced at his phone. "Staff meeting in fifteen minutes."

"On my schedule. I want to show you something first," Kate said.

He slid into the only chair in her office. "What's up?"

Kate grabbed her tote bag from under her desk and pulled out an envelope with the pictures from Susan McNally. She handed them to her brother, anxious for his reaction.

"Well, I'll be," Mitch said. A soft smile lit up his face. "Where did you get these?"

"Jess's mom. Yesterday."

"This is great, Bug. We don't have many pictures of the old days." He went through the pictures one by one. "Mom in high school. Wow. Look at those bell-bottom blue jeans." Mitch laughed and held up a photo. "That's TJ with Mom. They couldn't be more than seventeen." He turned the picture over. "Yeah, I'm right. The date is on the back."

"Why is it that you always call him TJ?" she asked.

"Tucker James. That's his name. He preferred to be called TJ. Said *dad* made him feel old."

"I called him *dad*."

"That was different. You were his little girl."

"Then why did he leave me?" There it was. Out there. The words she'd held bottled up inside of her for so many years.

Mitch released a breath and stared at her. The pain in his eyes mirrored the same pain in her heart. "TJ's leaving had nothing to do with you. I've told you that before."

"That's like telling me it wasn't personal. It was personal, Mitch. He was our father."

"TJ was a country boy who wasn't prepared for the responsibility of being a husband and a father. Think about it. He was eighteen when I was born." Mitch stared at the picture on top for a long moment. "Unless he was sidelined for an injury, the man was a guest in his own home, at best.

He was in and out of our lives as fast as an Oklahoma tornado."

Kate shook her head at the words. Math or not, she couldn't wrap her head around the notion that a father would leave his family. There had to have been something she could've done to make him stay.

Mitch shrugged. "He bolted when Mom went into hospice. It was as if her diagnosis threatened his mortality."

"Do you think that was it?"

Mitch gave a slow, thoughtful nod. "TJ Rainbolt was terrified, and that wasn't something any of us could fix."

A rap at the door had both Kate and Mitch turning.

"Sorry to interrupt, but Reece is bellowing for you two," Violet said with a grin.

"We'll be right there." Mitch handed the pictures back. "These are priceless. Maybe we'll make copies for everyone. What do you think?"

"Yes. That's a good idea." She stood, and Mitch put a hand on her shoulder.

"Bug, there was absolutely nothing you

could've done to stop him leaving. You were a kid."

"Where is he, Mitch?"

"TJ? I have no idea." He cocked his head and looked at her. "You haven't been looking, have you?"

Kate shoved the pictures in her desk drawer and grabbed her phone and a notebook. "Uh-oh. I hear Reece. We better hurry."

"Reece always bellows on Mondays," Mitch said. "It's part of his creative process."

She followed Mitch's long strides down the hall to the conference room where Reece sat at the head of the table. Mitch slid into the chair next to Reece.

Kate glanced around the table. The only empty chair was next to Jess. Lovely, because what she needed was another opportunity to interact with a guy who thought so little of her that he'd warned her away from his mother. She'd been chewing on his words for the last twenty-four hours, and they'd just served to sour her stomach.

When she sat down, her notebook slipped from her hands. They both reached for it, fingers colliding as their heads banged together.

"Great, now I'm giving you another concussion," Jess murmured.

"I'm fine," Kate muttered. "And with your hard head, I'm sure you're fine too." She snatched the notebook from his fingers and inched her chair away from his.

Jess offered a low chuckle. His gray eyes sparkled with mirth as they connected with hers. "Touché," he whispered, his voice low and husky.

Kate's gaze moved from his eyes to his mouth and then she quickly glanced away.

"First on today's agenda is the hoedown," Reece said. "We're three weeks out from Memorial Day, and then it's practically showtime." His gaze spanned the table, and he grinned. "First year in a long time that all the Rainbolts can participate. Tucker and Kate are both with us this year."

Kate had to admit she was excited about the event. Held a week after Memorial Day, the hoedown kicked off Rebel Ranch's summer. In the years since they'd established the guest ranch and started the tradition, Kate had missed only one.

Reece looked at her. "Kate, do you want to liaise with Chef Luna on the menu? Handle anything she needs."

"Me? No, thank you. Food is way out of my comfort zone."

Violet raised a hand. "I would love to do that this year."

"Done," Reece said while jotting on his laptop. "The band has been confirmed. Tents are on order." He looked up. "Willard, you're handling the generator and sound system?"

"Yes, sir. All confirmed."

"That's what I like to hear." He smiled. "We have guests joining us from Ballard Farm B&B this year, so I've rented a few golf carts to take them back and forth between properties. Mitch, do you have a few wranglers who can handle that?"

"Consider it done."

Reece's phone rang, and he grabbed the

cell from the table and stood. "Excuse me a moment, folks. Be right back."

Kate stared out the window at the blue May sky. While everyone checked their phones and laptops, she sat entranced by the wind dancing through the lush green leaves of the maple trees. It was the first week of May already. She'd been here almost three weeks.

Where was Franny right now? Probably still home in Texas, practicing and getting geared up for the summer rodeos. She'd start out slow and then hit it hard during Cowboy Christmas, the big-prize-money period at the end of June and beginning of July. That meant endless stretches of highway.

Kate missed her rodeo life, though not the miles of empty road. Or the loneliness. But she sure pined for the freedom. Getting accustomed to a desk job was a lot harder than she'd thought it would be.

She stood, walked over to a window and cranked it open. Immediately, a breeze kicked into the room. It smelled like hay and sunshine.

"That's nice, Miss Kate," Willard said. "Just what we needed."

She slipped into her chair without glancing at Jess.

"It's always something, isn't it?" Reece said minutes later when he returned to the room. He looked at the open window, perplexed, and then opened his laptop again.

"Everything okay?" Mitch asked.

"It will be. Willard, I need you to put out another fire. The manager over at Ballard Farm has had to leave. His father is ill. I'm going to need you to take charge of things there. Meet with Asa and Nan Turner and ensure they have enough help in the orchards and at the produce stand. Then check in with my wife and see if she needs any assistance with the final stage of the renovation. The first guests check in next weekend."

"I can do that. What about the guest stable?" Willard asked. "I've stepped in to assist Jess until Miss Kate is ready."

"It's a real problem that you're so talented," Mitch said. He stood and poured a cup of coffee from the back counter.

"Ain't it the truth," the old cowboy said with a laugh. "I was scheduled to go to look at a couple of horses with Jess tomorrow."

Reece's gaze landed on Kate. "Kate, do you mind going with Jess?" He paused.

"Me?" She tamped back her excitement at this turn of events when she realized Jess figured into the equation. "Why not send Finn with Jess?"

"He's teaching at OSU with Tucker all week. Besides, this will give Jess some time to bring you up to speed on what's going on with the equine program."

"Because?" she prompted.

"Because if you're good with it, you can oversee behind the scenes—inventory, supplies, scheduling, staff training—until Willard is back or you get a medical clearance. Assign the staff to handle the hands-on aspects with the animals."

She didn't point out that she could have been doing that all along if Jess hadn't convinced them that she'd start running with scissors the first chance she got. Instead, she kept her mouth shut and bit back excitement as she flipped through her notebook. She didn't want to seem too eager or they might change their minds, and she desperately needed an opportunity to spend more time out of her closet office.

"Um, sure, I can move a few things around and do that if it will help you out."

"Jess, that work for you?" Reece asked.

"You're the boss." His voice gave nothing away. Kate didn't really want to know his opinion on the subject, so she kept her gaze focused on her brother.

"Kate, that reminds me," Violet said. "The forms from human resources have arrived for you to sign. We need to get your insurance coverage started."

"I'll have medical insurance?" She looked from Violet to Reece.

"Of course. All full-time employees receive benefits after thirty days. Even a 401k plan," Violet said.

Kate grinned. The morning was definitely looking up. She'd gotten a pass to leave the bookkeeping closet as needed, and she had benefits coming if she decided to stick around. The only downside was Jess.

When the meeting was over, Kate stood and stretched. When she turned, Jess stood in her way. "Was there something?"

"Yeah. Tomorrow. I'll drive."

Kate opened her mouth to argue and decided against it. His vehicle had all the bells and whistles. It would be silly to protest, though she longed to on principle. She nodded.

"Six o'clock work for you?"

"Six? The sun will be pouring its first cup of coffee at six. What's the rush?"

"We have two stops. The first one is a two-hour drive from here, and I don't want to lose the entire day. You can always sleep in the truck."

"Fine. I'll be there." She wasn't happy about getting up so early or being cloistered in a truck cab with Jess for four hours minimum. But she'd be there, saying a prayer of thanks and doing her best not to expect the other boot to fall.

"Beautiful horse," Jess said. He dismounted the paint and handed the reins to the stable manager. "Thank you. I'll send our vet out of course, but we'd like to purchase those two if the vet check is good."

The other cowboy nodded and shook Jess's hand. Then he walked across the yard to where Kate leaned against the split rail corral fence. The breeze whipped her long dark hair across her face, and he couldn't help but notice how beautiful she was. His chest tightened, and he looked away.

"Did you see that view?" she asked when he joined her.

He followed her gaze to where a line of tall conifers in the distance reached so high that they seemed to meet the azure sky.

"You can see forever from here. I guess it's because the town is on a small plateau."

Jess was surprised by her words. She'd been almost monosyllabic since he'd picked her up this morning. His penance for Sunday at his mother's, he figured. He regretted his harsh words, though he hadn't found an opportunity to apologize.

She plucked a blade of sweet grass and put it in her mouth while looking around. "I wouldn't mind running a stable," Kate said.

"You'll be doing that at Rebel Ranch if you decide to stick around."

"I mean my own place."

"Rebel is your own place." He dug in his pockets for his keys.

"It's Reece and Mitch's place."

"Only because you haven't claimed it as your own." He nodded toward the truck. "Ready?"

"Yes. Let's get going."

Once they'd settled in the truck, Jess pulled out the paperwork on the horses they'd seen today from a folder on the dash and handed the sheets to Kate. "What did you think?"

"The paints were very calm, approachable. That mare especially. Notice how she put up her ears when you entered the corral? She likes people. That's just what we need with the number of nervous riders that check into the guest ranch. I have a solid gut feeling about the place too."

Jess agreed. He'd taken time to ride the horses at both stables, but his instinct said the registered paints at this second stop checked off all the boxes. They'd be a good addition to Rebel Ranch. Once they passed a vet exam, he'd recommend the sale proceed.

"Looks like we agree." Jess pulled on his seat belt and checked his phone for messages. It was nearly noon, but they'd visited both stables, and he was happy to return to the ranch as soon as possible instead of sitting in a truck cab with a woman who smelled like mangoes and messed with his mind and his disposition.

"Mind if we stop in town for something to eat before we head back?" Kate asked. "I'm starving."

"You're hungry?"

"Yes. It's lunchtime." When he didn't respond, she continued. "You know lunch. The meal between breakfast and dinner."

"Yeah, sure. I suppose so." He slipped on his sunglasses, backed up the truck and headed for the main road through town.

"If it's going to be a hardship for you, then maybe we can stop at the 7-Eleven for some donut gems and a frozen rainbow Slurpee."

"I said we could stop for lunch. No more donut powder all over my seats, if you don't mind."

"It's a truck."

"Yeah. A truck I'm still paying for."

She was silent, staring out the window, ignoring him as they entered the city limits of Plume, Oklahoma, a town that boasted a population of five thousand. A shiny silver police cruiser waited for them as they approached the twenty-five-miles-an-hour speed limit sign somewhat obstructed by a large maple tree.

Fortunately, Jess was familiar with this particular speed trap. Plume would not be taking his money today. He'd already slowed down long before the sign appeared.

"Oh, look," Kate said as a billboard came into view. "Catfish special. I love catfish. Don't you?"

"Not really. They're bottom feeders."

"So are halibut, flounder, cod and sole." She shook her head. "I suppose you have something against fried okra and hushpuppies too?"

"Not a fan, as a matter of fact."

She huffed and shook her head. "And you call yourself an Okie?"

"Actually, up until two months ago, I called myself a Montanan."

"What do they have in Montana that's so great?"

"Peace and quiet."

Kate opened her mouth and closed it. She reached for the plastic grocery bag at her feet, rustling wrappers as she examined the contents.

"They say you really get to know someone when you take a road trip," Jess murmured.

"Are you about to insult me?" Kate asked.

He glanced at the plastic bag. "I've never seen anyone eat so much."

"I have a good metabolism." She shot him a lethal glare. "And it wasn't that much."

"A banana. An apple. Two granola bars. Trail mix and peanut butter crackers."

"It was a long ride."

"Not that long."

"Are you trying to be disagreeable?" she asked. "Because you're doing a great job."

Jess laughed in spite of himself. "I guess I just remembered you differently."

She straightened in her seat. "Pull over. Just pull over. I want catfish, and if you keep talking, I'm really going to get mad and say something you'll regret, and then I might not get my lunch, which would be a real shame."

"Hold your horses. We're there." Jess pulled the truck into a spot in front of Lucy-Mae's Café and removed his seat belt. Kate was out of the truck in a heartbeat and struggling to pull open the heavy glass door with one arm before his boots hit the asphalt.

"Hang on a minute, would you?" he asked. She was silent as he held the door.

"Welcome, folks. I'm Lucy-Mae. Would you like a booth or a table?" A middle-aged woman with red glasses, rolled-up blue jeans and a Gailard Sartain T-shirt greeted them. She waved a hand around the busy room.

"Booth, please," Jess said.

Lucy-Mae led them to a booth with a window view. A frown crossed her face as she assessed Kate's cast and then glared at Jess. "Honey, how did you manage to break your arm?"

"She wrestled a bull," Jess said. "Ask her."

The woman assessed Kate, and her eyes widened. "Are you that female rodeo clown that sits in those barrels?" She cocked her head. "I do believe you are. I pack up my dogs and my husband and point the RV in the direction of Tucson every winter. We always go to the rodeo. I saw you in the arena in February." The grin that lit up her face was as wide as her hips. "What are the odds? A real live hero in my café."

"I was just doing my job," Kate murmured. Pink crept from her neck to her face as she picked up the plastic menu.

"Sweetie, you saved Beau Connor's life. You're a hero. A real hero."

Kate looked at him and then away as Lucy-Mae whipped out an order pad and pulled a pen from her bosom.

"What'll you have? It's on the house."

At the mention of food, Kate smiled and pointed to the chalkboard on the wall. "The catfish special, please. With slaw, hush puppies, baked beans, corn bread and extra fried okra."

"See, I knew you were a sharp gal the moment I laid eyes on you." She turned to Jess. "And what'll your boyfriend have?"

Kate sputtered. "He's not my boyfriend. He's my boss."

"Humph. His loss. I have a grandson I'd like you to meet." She wagged a finger at

Kate. "He's out of town, but you tell me next time you pass through, you hear?"

"Yes, ma'am."

Jess studied the menu while ignoring the exchange. He was outnumbered here, and after annoying Kate in the truck, he'd keep his thoughts to himself. Later on, he'd think about why the idea of Lucy-Mae fixing Kate up with her grandson put a burr under his saddle.

"Coffee with your lunch, young lady?" Lucy-Mae asked.

"Yes, please."

"I'd like water," Jess said.

Lucy-Mae turned to leave.

"Excuse me," Jess called. "You didn't get my order."

She swiveled on a sneaker and looked at him over the rim of her glasses. "What'll it be, boss man?"

"The Okie burger. Medium rare. With fries. Please."

Lucy-Mae laughed. "Cook is color-blind, so you get what you get. I recommend the catfish."

"I'll take my chances with the burger. Thanks."

"Good to live dangerously." She paused and looked through him to Kate. "I'll be back in a jiffy with coffee, sweetie."

"She's a character," Kate said with a grin.

"I'll say. How come you never mentioned that Beau Connor was the bull rider that day?"

"I wasn't focused on the rider. The bull's name was Despiadado."

"That's impressive."

"The bull or the rider?"

"Come on. Beau Connor? Even I know who he is."

Kate frowned and reached for the dessert menu propped up behind the hot sauce. "So I was foolhardy until you heard it was Beau Connor in the arena with me?"

"No. I didn't say that. I'm just surprised, that's all. He's a legend."

"It doesn't matter to me who the rider is. I take my job very seriously."

Jess gave a slow shake of his head. "Man, I need to start wearing my old boots when

I'm around you because it seems all I do is step in it left and right."

A minute later, Lucy-Mae was back with a carafe in one hand and two mugs dangling from her fingers. "Here you go. Cream and sugar are on the table."

He stared with surprise as their hostess retreated. "I guess I'm drinking coffee." There was no response from Kate, who slowly stirred cream and sugar into her mug.

Jess searched for something to engage her and get them over the awkward silence between them. "What do you think about taking over some of the equine duties?"

She cocked her head. "You know I'm excited. Besides, have you seen my office? I hyperventilate every time the door accidentally closes. Since it used to be a closet, when the door closes, the lights turn off."

He tried not to laugh. "Won't be too long before your cast is off."

"So you say. I feel like a five-year-old on a road trip. Are we there yet? I keep looking at the calendar, and it's still weeks until my appointment."

"Mitch put together a manual for all the supervisory positions on the ranch. The one for the equine manager position is very comprehensive. I'll get you a copy when we get back."

Kate smiled. "I am not surprised Mitch did that. He was the one who alphabetized the cans in our cupboard."

"Maybe you should use this time to figure out how you want to manage things once you take over."

"Manage things? What's to figure out? You just said that Mitch put together a bible. So what is there? Employee schedules. Vet visits. Guest training and safety. Ordering supplies. It's not rocket science. Sounds simple enough."

"You're looking at this all wrong."

"Am I?" She sipped her coffee and closed her eyes, savoring the brew. "That's good coffee."

"Ah, yeah," he said, momentarily distracted by the dreamy expression on her face. "What I mean is that you should ask yourself what you can offer the program at the ranch. How can you put your stamp on things? Make it your own?"

She frowned and cocked her head. "Make it my own?"

"You come from a distinctly unique background with experience that no one else on the ranch has. Put your touch on the equine program. Something that says Kate Rainbolt. Maybe something that Reece can put in that fancy color brochure or on the web page."

For a long minute, she simply stared at him. "Why are you telling me this?" She narrowed her eyes and leaned back against the booth. "I thought you wanted me as far from the stables as possible. Preferably in another county."

Good question. Why was he sharing with her as though they were friends? He shrugged and reached for the obvious response. One that didn't involve thinking too hard about his motivation. "I don't want to see you injured again."

She stared at him silently, as though measuring his words. He sensed the moment she put her shield down and relaxed, and he realized this was it—the opening he'd been waiting for. An opportunity to apologize. He found himself gun-shy, though, afraid she'd kick his apology back at him, as he'd been mulling for days and well-deserved.

"And look, Kate, about Sunday. You were right. I was out of line."

She bit her lip and nodded, listening.

"I'm dealing with my own issues and sometimes…" He shrugged. "Sometimes they get the upper hand. I wasn't there for my mother when my father died."

"I thought it was sudden. A heart attack?" She cocked her head, eyes questioning. "Surely, you don't blame yourself because you were in Montana."

He paused, not sure he was ready to voice aloud the guilt that he carried due to the infrequent visits home because of the rocky relationship between him and his father.

"Look," he finally said, "I just don't want

to let my mother down again. So maybe I'm a little overprotective."

"You think I'm going to let her down," Kate said. She blinked, and her jaw sagged.

Jess jerked back at her words. "That's not what I meant."

"That's what you said."

"I've got both boots in my mouth, and this isn't coming out the way it should."

Lucy-Mae interrupted the discussion when she appeared with a large tray filled with their orders and dispensed the plates. "Here you go. Enjoy. We've got a great pecan pie when you're done."

"Thank you," Kate murmured.

"Honey, you okay?" Lucy-Mae asked. She shot Jess a disapproving glance.

"I'm fine." Kate smiled down at the plate that was overflowing with catfish and sides. "This is wonderful. Thank you."

Jess picked up his knife as an awkward silence stretched between them. He cut his burger in half and grimaced at the chunk of leather that rested on a poppy seed bun.

"Mind if I ask what your plans are?" Kate asked.

"My plans?" He stared at his plate.

"Are you going back to Montana when your mother is better?"

"The only thing that's going to make my mother better is a kidney transplant. She's on the UNOS list, but wait times are longer for people over fifty."

"UNOS?"

"United Network for Organ Sharing."

Kate nodded. "I assume you've considered donating a kidney yourself?"

"Yeah, of course. Both Nicole and I were tested. But our physician recommends against the surgery because we're both at high risk for kidney disease."

"We should pray about this," Kate said. "Now, before my catfish gets cold."

He stiffened. "Do you think I haven't been praying?"

"Stand down, cowboy. I'm saying that the two of us praying together, well, there's a little extra juice in those prayers." She held out her free hand. "The Bible says so."

Jess took her hand though he doubted the wisdom of such an action. For a moment, he tumbled back in time to when they'd last held hands, and he had to work to focus on the final words of the sweet prayer Kate uttered.

"Lord, You've got Your hands on this situation, and we thank You for taking care of Jess's mom. Amen."

"Amen."

Kate pulled her hand free to grab a fork. "That burger looks terrible. Do you want to split my lunch?"

"I'm fine. I went into this with my eyes open." He reached for the steak sauce. "Thanks for praying."

"Anytime. I happen to like your mother. You, I only tolerate."

Jess chuckled. "There you go. That's the Kate I know so well."

Chapter Six

"Hey, boss, the horses are here." Willard popped his head into Jess's office.

"Thanks. Where are they?" Grateful for the interruption, he lifted his head. Lately, his job had far more paperwork than he preferred.

"Finn is doing a preliminary check in the corral." Willard smiled. "They sure are pretty."

"Yeah, they are. Have you seen Kate anywhere?"

"Nope. Then again, I only just got here."

"Wait, aren't you supposed to be at Ballard Farm?"

"Yes, sir, I'm here returning Baby."

"What? That cow isn't supposed to get loose anymore. Those are new fences."

"I'll tell Baby that right away." Willard chuckled as he left.

Jess stood and stretched, stepping away from the computer. He'd been working on the June schedule for the ranch wranglers for hours and was stiff. His staff would handle the trail rides and campouts, along with moving the cattle between grazing spaces. Everything that said "authentic Western experience" for the ranch guests.

The bright spot the last two weeks had been working with Kate. Despite her jocular attitude, she was diligent about her duties. He hadn't expected anything less, and her focus on the job also meant somewhat less awkwardness and animosity between them. It was a small step forward, and he'd take that over her avoiding him.

He wasn't sure what sort of relationship he wanted with Kate, didn't dare to think about it, but maybe friendship was in their future.

From the tack room, he heard Kate's

voice. It sounded like she was talking to Einstein. A few minutes later, the clanging of a feed bucket sounded, as though it had fallen on the ground, and the horse's loud whinny of distress echoed through the building.

Jess raced toward the sound and found Einstein's stall door open. The horse whinnied again, clearly upset. Jess's breath caught in his throat at the sight of Kate leaning against the stall slats with a hand to her head. "Kate. Are you okay?"

"I think so."

"Did you fall?"

"Not really. I got a little dizzy, that's all." She struggled to straighten, and when their eyes met, he saw fear in the depths of hers.

Jess gently put his arm around her shoulders to assist, avoiding her casted arm. "Then you fell."

"Against the slats. Not on the ground. Relax."

"Relax? You could have passed out and been trampled." He worked to calm down and tuck away the lecture he was ready to deliver until he was certain she was really all right. "Why isn't Einstein turned out?"

"He's got a farrier appointment. Einstein has a long-toe issue. I like to keep his farrier visits a little more frequent than usual."

"That doesn't explain why you're in the stall." His eyes were level with hers, and he refused to look away until he got an answer that might make his heart rate slow down.

"I was pitching in. Someone called in sick."

"Kate Rainbolt, what am I going to do with you?"

"Not a thing. I am not your responsibility."

"When you're on the job, you are." He released a frustrated breath. "You can't keep on like this, Kate. You aren't alone in this world. People care about you. You're being selfish."

He'd promised himself he wasn't going to do it, but after talking with Lucy-Mae at the diner, he'd ignored his own sound advice and had gone home and searched the internet for videos of Kate's accident. The images were seared into his mind. Now he was more determined than ever that she would not get injured on his watch.

"What did your doctor say about the dizzy spells?" The question came out more harshly than he'd intended.

"She referred me to a neurologist."

"And?"

"I haven't been yet." Once again, her gaze met his, but this time, she looked away. "Don't say it."

"Seriously? Why not? Kate, you've been working at the ranch for how long now?"

"I've been busy." She ran a hand through her hair.

He glanced at his watch. "As it happens, as a physician's son, I know a lot of doctors and even a neurologist. Uncle Bobby works at the neurology clinic in Broken Arrow. I'm calling him now."

"Uncle Bobby? Please. That sounds like a cartoon character, not a neurologist." She stroked Einstein's flank and then his ears. "Sorry to scare you, baby."

"Uncle Bobby is an honorary uncle. Went to med school with my dad."

"I see."

"No, you don't. But that's okay. He's a nice guy. You'll like him."

Her head jerked toward him. "Wait. Wait. You aren't calling him now, are you?"

"I sure am. You stay right here and don't move."

Jess stepped into his office to make the call and easily pulled in a favor. When he returned to Kate, she was sitting on a bale of hay, a frown on her face as he approached.

"As a special favor to his favorite almost nephew, he's going to fit you in at the end of the day. I gave him Dr. Bowie's phone number so your records can be sent over."

"Today?"

"Yeah, today. He says to bring your lab work and any imaging results you have." Jess looked at her. "You have that stuff?"

"Oh, I have plenty of that stuff. I could wallpaper a restroom with my paperwork."

Jess shook his head. Of course she did, and if he hadn't stepped in today, she would've avoided the neurology consult forever.

"Why are you looking at me like that?" she asked.

"We can discuss it later." He glanced at his watch. "You have time to shower before we head out. I'll pick you up at your house in thirty minutes."

"I—"

"Thirty minutes, Kate. I pulled in a big favor here."

"Okay, fine. I'll go, but I don't need anyone to take me."

"Either I take you, or I chat with Mitch." Though Kate's eyes rounded with outrage, it gave him little pleasure to win this small battle. It was the right thing to do. He told himself he was doing it only for the Rainbolts, and he almost believed that was the truth.

"You've gotten a lot more stubborn in the last ten years," she huffed. "Mean-spirited too."

"That's because I'm no longer a love-struck kid following you around." He grimaced. It pained him that Willard was right in his assessment. Ten years ago, he'd been so in love he hadn't been able to see beyond that. If he had, he would have realized that Kate had given him plenty of warnings. She'd told him she wanted to find her father and nothing would stand in her way. Not even him.

Too late, he'd found out that she'd meant what she said.

That wouldn't happen this go-round.

An hour and a half later, they were in Broken Arrow, Oklahoma, and he was cooling his heels in the lobby of Uncle Bobby's office. After Kate's name was called, he left and drove over to the Bass Pro Shop Outdoor World and wandered around until she texted that she was done.

Kate was waiting on the sidewalk when he pulled the truck into a parking spot. He got out and opened the passenger door.

"That didn't take long," she said with a chipper smile. "Ready to head back?"

Jess jumped into the driver's seat and faced her. "Nice try. We had a deal. You tell me what Uncle Bobby said, and I'll maybe keep my mouth shut."

"Fine. No bullfighting."

"Well, lookee there, I'm not the only one who doesn't think jumping in front of bulls is a smart move."

"Maybe you should have been a doctor."

He paused at the stinging words. "That was a low blow. Even for you, Kate."

"I'm so sorry." Eyes downcast, she released a breath. "I wasn't referring to your dad. It was a randomly rude comment, and I apologize."

"Apology accepted. What else did Uncle Bobby say?"

"He did another CT and looked at the MRI results from Tucson. No change in the fracture."

"And horseback riding?"

"Once the cast is off, he'll okay me to ride Einstein if I use full safety precautions and schedule vestibular training."

"Vestibular? Meaning?"

"Something to do with the inner ear. There's a therapist in Pawhuska he recommended, so I won't need to drive to Tulsa."

"That's all?"

"He mentioned getting plenty of sleep

and increasing breaks when I'm working on the computer."

A silence settled between them as Jess digested the words.

"You have to tell your brothers," he finally said.

"There's nothing to tell." She shrugged. "The doctor said it should resolve with therapy. Until there is evidence to the contrary, I'm fine."

Fine. Kate's mantra.

"And what about returning to the rodeo?"

She released a breath. "Yes, well, he recommends against any sport that is high risk for repeat concussion. He thinks I've likely been concussed before, and the risk of TBI is high."

"TBI?"

"Traumatic brain injury."

Traumatic brain injury. Jess was stunned and stared at Kate, waiting for her reaction. After all, she'd just been given a serious medical diagnosis and been told her career was over. But she only stared out the window, chin high.

"You're awfully calm about this," he said.

"Am I?" Kate turned toward him and toyed with the paperwork in her hands. "I guess it hasn't really sunk in yet." She paused. "One minute, I'm getting my blood pressure checked, and the next, I'm looking at a giant picture of my brain and Uncle Bobby is saying things like depression, anger, memory loss and suicidal ideation..." Her lashes fluttered closed for a moment, shielding her eyes as she released a slow breath.

She was in shock, and he couldn't blame her.

"I'm sorry, Kate," he said softly.

"Not half as sorry as I am," she murmured. "I thought I'd be falling down and getting up and rodeoing forever. That's pretty silly, right? Thirty years old, and I'm back to wondering what I want to be when I grow up."

"It's not silly. This is a lot to handle all at once."

She looked at him. "Stop being nice to me. I've been a total brat toward you."

"Yeah, you have. But I'm not holding it against you, because you're dealing with some heavy stuff right now."

"That's awfully mature of you."

He shrugged. "I'm a mature kind of guy."

Big blue eyes stared up at him, and it was all he could do not to hold her close.

"You ready to head back to the ranch?" he asked.

"No. Not yet," she said. "Could we maybe go for a coffee?"

Jess didn't let himself think about the half dozen things he needed to attend to at the ranch. Instead, he nodded. "Sure."

"We passed one of those chains a block over. I could go for double something, high in caffeine and calories with a side of zero-nutritional-value pastries."

Jess laughed as the tension eased from him. "Let's go."

He nursed a plain coffee while Kate chased the whipped cream in her plastic tumbler with a straw. She frowned the entire time, deep in thought.

"You sure are quiet. Are you thinking about what Uncle Bobby said?"

"Does it matter?"

"Everything matters."

"I'm thinking that I don't have a plan. For the first time in my life, I have no discernable direction."

"Don't think about the rest of your life. Start small. How about Memorial Day? Got any plans for the three-day weekend? It's coming up here soon."

"I'm supposed to go to Tucker's new house on that Saturday. They're hosting a little Memorial Day family thing, but I'm pretty sure I'm going to play hooky." She looked at him. "What about you?"

"Nothing much. Nicole and my mom are driving to Porter. My dad's sister invited the family for a barbecue."

"And you're going?"

"I haven't decided." Wrapping his hands around his mug, he eyed Kate, unsure if he should pursue the topic but unable to resist. "What sort of playing hooky are you going to get into?"

"Rodeo. What else?"

He shook his head, disappointed with the answer. "You've spent your adult life at the rodeo."

"The thrill never fades. Besides, this one is special. It's the Decker Stampede down Route 66. It's held Memorial Day weekend."

"Yeah, I know. That's been going on for like seventy years."

"Do you want to go with me? Maybe Sunday? If we can be friends, and maybe not snipe at each other for a few hours, that is."

She was inviting him to spend the day with her? Jess mulled the offer, trying not to show surprise at the invitation. If he had a lick of sense, he'd say no. Trouble was, sense went out the door when it came to Kate.

"Well?" she prompted.

"I can't promise about the sniping." He looked at her. "But I'm willing to give it a shot."

A small smile lit up her face. "Great, because I don't think I'm ready to face my family. They'll grill me over whether or not I'm staying in Rebel or hitting the road again." She sighed. "I have no idea what I'm going to do with the rest of my life. I'm a has-been rodeo cowgirl with nothing to show for my life but a cat, a horse and a disreputable truck."

"Kate, I could say the same thing. I've been working ten years on someone else's ranch." As the words slipped from his mouth, their truth sideswiped him. Were they in the same place?

"Do you want your own ranch?" she asked.

"I don't know anymore. My plan was to work with my uncle, eventually buy into a partnership. Moving back to Oklahoma has shuffled my priorities. I don't know what the future holds at this point."

"I guess we've both been thrown for a loop," she said.

Jess nodded.

As if in silent agreement, they both stood. Depositing his cup in the trash, Jess led the way out the door.

"At least you have a nice truck," Kate

said as they approached his dually. "Way nicer than mine."

"That I will agree with." He opened the door for her. "Where did you get your rust bucket?"

"I won her." She smiled, really smiled, for the first time since he'd found her in Einstein's stall. The sweet expression on her face made him long to keep her smiling.

Jess got in the truck and pulled on his seat belt. "You won the truck?"

"Yes. Not like in gambling. I literally won the truck. I was at a little rodeo in Houston and placed first in the barrel racing competition, but there wasn't enough prize money, so they gave me the truck."

"That's no prize."

"At the time, I was thrilled."

He wrapped his hands around the steering wheel and looked at her. Had they bridged the tension in their relationship today? Would she hear what he had to say without putting up walls again? "Let's get serious here for a minute, Kate. When we get back to Rebel, you need to talk to your family."

"Jess, I am serious. You leveraged me into going to the neurologist and listened to me whine and then agreed to go to a rodeo with me. For that, I am grateful. But I don't need another brother."

"I'm not applying for the job." Nope. Far from it. Right now he was doing his best to fight feelings that were far, far from brotherly.

"Good, and just so you know, I will continue to circumvent the truth in an effort to keep my brothers from further pain."

"Circumventing the truth is the cousin to lying, and you know I won't lie."

"Jess, I am not telling them about this visit. Nor will you." She sighed. "What happens in Jess's truck stays in Jess's truck. Couldn't we go with that?"

He bit back a laugh. This was pure Kate. Some things never changed. "I'll think about it," he said.

"Think hard, please."

Oh, yeah, he'd be thinking hard. Thinking hard about why he'd gotten himself tangled up in her life again. Willingly. If he didn't know better, he'd think he was the one who'd hit his head.

Kate listened to her voice mail and glanced at the calendar. Dr. Bowie's office had confirmed her upcoming appointment for an X-ray and possible cast removal. Soon, she'd be a free woman.

Maybe she'd plan a little celebration with Bella. Takeout from the Arrowhead Diner for herself and a can of highbrow cat food for Bella. The expensive, organic stuff with lots of gravy. Then they'd watch *The Aristocats*. Bella's favorite movie.

Her cell rang, and she reached for it, grinning when she saw it was Franny.

"Kate, how you doing?"

"Great. Absolutely great. I just found out my cast is coming off early if the X-ray says I've been a good bone knitter. So say a prayer for good knitting, will you?"

"You've got it. This is the best news I've heard all week."

"Thanks, Franny." She smiled. "It sure is nice to hear your voice. How's Rex? What's going on down in the panhandle?"

"Nothing new with the husband. I'm getting a little cabin fever. Anxious to get back on the road before I do something foolish like clean the house."

"That could be dangerous."

"Right?" Franny chuckled. "Oh, and I lost another assistant. But what else is new? They see a bright shiny object or a handsome cowboy, and off they go into the sunset."

Kate laughed.

"So what I guess I'm trying to say is that I have an opening in my crew. I need someone to take care of my horses on the road, manage the books. You know, the front-end work."

"You want to hire me?"

"I thought it might be a way for you to ease back in. And if your cast is coming off soon, this sounds like perfect timing, right?"

Kate sat down at the kitchen table, taken

aback by the offer that had come on the heels of the neurologist's diagnosis.

Ease back in.

Kate rolled the words around in her head. Did she want to ease back in to rodeo life, or would a clean break be better for her mental health? Being Franny's assistant meant she'd still be part of the circuit, just not in the arena anymore.

From barrel racing to riding the barrel to sitting in the bleachers. Quite a fall from grace. The ache in her heart at this turn of events hadn't dulled since she'd seen the neurologist, but was this a door opening or a misstep?

"You sure are thinking hard," Franny said.

"What sort of timeline are you talking about?" Kate asked.

"We'd be pulling out of Texas in time to hit as many Christmas rodeos as possible."

"Early June. Franny, June is within spitting distance, my friend."

She laughed. "So it is. Now you see how muddled I am. Juggling everything has me unsure if I'm coming or going."

"I have a hoedown here at the ranch I'm committed to the weekend after Memorial Day." Kate sighed.

"Hey, hey, don't stress this," Franny said. "Tie things up. Pray on it."

"Yes. That's exactly what I need to do."

"There's a small local rodeo here in June. Maybe you could come down for a visit, and we can talk."

"I'll call you, Franny. Promise." Kate disconnected the phone and sat staring out the window. Normally, she'd be jumping at the opportunity. But now... Now her stomach was in knots. She had one boot in a past that would take her nowhere and the other in an uncertain future.

Something touched her arm, and Kate looked down to see a gray paw patting her gently and big green eyes staring at her.

Bella started walking down the hall. She paused and glanced back at Kate over her shoulder.

"I'm coming. I'm coming." Kate followed until Bella stopped in front of her food dish in the kitchen. Her empty food dish.

Seriously? This was a smart cat.

From the cupboard, Kate pulled a can of the wet food Tucker had recommended and opened it. She put half in the dish and mushed it around. Bella wasted no time digging in.

Kate glanced around the kitchen, realizing she was hungry too. The Eagle Donuts box was empty, and the only cereal left was bran flakes. She pulled eggs from the fridge and heated a frying pan on the stove. Anyone could cook eggs. Right?

Cracking two into a bowl *was* easy. Whipping them and holding the bowl with her arm in a long cast? Not so easy. The only bread she had was in the freezer and hard as a rock, so she stuck it in the toaster and inched up the dial.

When her phone rang, she turned and scooped it up from the kitchen table.

"Hey, Kate, it's Nicole. I am so sorry to bother you, but I can't reach Jess. I'm pretty sure this is his weekend to work at the ranch."

"It is. He had a trail ride with some guests

early today. Sometimes calls drop between the house and north pasture."

"Oh, I guess I'll try again in a little bit. Thanks."

The tremor in Jess's sister's voice gave Kate pause. "Nicole? Is everything okay?"

"I'm in the emergency room with my mother. She's going to be admitted for IV fluids, and I hate to leave her, but I need to pick up Olive at a friend's. She's not feeling well." Nicole sighed. "One of those days already."

"Oh, my. That's not good," Kate said. "I'd offer to get Olive, but I'm sure she'd rather have you there. Why don't I come and sit with your mother?" It was the least she could do for a woman who'd done so much for the Rainbolts.

"Are you sure?" Nicole asked.

"Absolutely. Which hospital?"

"Pawhuska Hospital. Her electrolytes are off, so they're going to keep her overnight."

"Not a problem. I'll head there now. You go ahead and get Olive."

"Thank you so much."

Kate searched in the dryer for matching socks and tugged them on before remembering the eggs on the stove. By then, the distinct smell of burning toast wafted into the laundry room.

"No. No. No." She raced into the kitchen, where a dark cloud ascended from the toaster toward the ceiling. When the smoke detector began to trill, Bella shot out of the room.

"Coward," Kate muttered. Unplugging the toaster, she dumped the contents into the soapy water in the sink before turning on the ceiling fan and cracking a window. She feared the appliance would never be the same again. A glance at the stove confirmed the demise of the eggs.

For a moment, Kate stood in the kitchen, surveying the disaster before resetting the smoke detector. She grabbed a box of cookies from the cupboard, picked up her purse and headed out the door.

By the time she arrived at the Pawhuska hospital, Susan McNally had been settled in a room. She sat up in bed with IV pumps on either side of her and smiled. "This line is my breakfast, and I think that one is lunch," the older woman joked.

Kate told her about her own breakfast attempt, which had Susan laughing.

"You must be her daughter," the nurse said as she sailed into the room with a cup of pills.

"No. Just a friend."

"If you'd married Jess, you'd have been a daughter," Susan said.

Kate's eyes rounded, and she looked away for a moment. She couldn't deny that she'd thought a time or two about how different her life would be today if she'd said yes to Jess's proposal. But every time she'd started wondering, she'd immediately buried the idea. If only she could have had it all, but she'd chosen to try to find her past before she considered a future.

Susan put a hand on Kate's shoulder. "I'm still holding out for that to happen. After all the time that's passed, here you both are, back in Rebel. That can't be coincidence."

"I, um…" Kate searched for a gentle response. "Jess and I are only friends. You know that, right?"

"Maybe so, but when he looks at you… Well, his face says something else."

"Indigestion?" Kate suggested.

Susan laughed. "That's what I like about you. You have such a sense of humor. Jess is so serious and arrow straight. You shake things up, Kate. He needs that."

"I'm not so sure Jess appreciates my sense of humor," Kate murmured.

"You know, you have your momma's wit. She never let life get her down, no matter how dark the day."

Kate perked up and found herself once again thirsty for bits of information about her mother. It was as if with the recent loss of her husband, Susan understood how desperately Kate needed to fill in the puzzle pieces of her heritage. Kate was grateful and silently vowed she'd find a way to thank Jess's mother for her kindness and generosity.

They chatted for a while, until Susan's

eyes began to drift closed. Kate sat listening to the clock ticking as the IV dripped drop by drop into Susan's tubing. Yes, she'd be home soon, but hospital admission was a temporary fix at best. Her mother's best friend needed more than this. Deserved more than this.

She stood and walked into the hallway, silently gathering courage as she approached the nursing station where Susan's nurse stood typing into a computer.

"Excuse me."

The nurse turned. "Yes. Can I help you?"

"I hope so. I'd like to find out about kidney donations. Can you point me in the right direction?"

"Sure. There's a screening process, and if that's a go, it's followed by a day of medical tests." She opened a drawer and handed Kate a brochure. "I suggest you go online and check out the Donor Care Network. Then touch base with your medical provider. They will refer you to specialists who can get things started."

"Thanks." She walked back to Susan's

room and sat in the chair once again.
"Lord," she prayed quietly, "show me Your
will here."

"Kate."

She looked up to find Jess in the doorway. Worry was etched on his handsome
face, and her heart clutched at the sight.

With a finger to her lips, Kate nodded
toward the hall. She shoved the brochure
she'd been reading into her purse and met
him outside the room.

"Have you talked with your mom's
nurse?" she asked.

He nodded. "Yeah."

"Then let's get some coffee." She glanced
at the signs as they walked down the hall.
"This is a small hospital."

"Twenty-five beds, last time I checked.
Mom usually goes to Tulsa. But this is a
great place when she can't get there."

Kate grabbed powdered donut gems
along with a large coffee and followed Jess
to a table.

"I'm so sorry you had to spend your time
off here," he said. "This was Nicole's day

to be on call for Mom, and I was out of cell range."

"You can't be held responsible for poor cell coverage."

"I understand in theory, but that doesn't mean much when I can't be counted on."

"Well, as a wise man once said, it's good to let others help you."

"Wise man. Right." He shook his head. "It was really great of you to come, especially since I'm guessing you've had your fill of hospitals."

"That's the truth. I break out in hives when I see gelatin squares." She broke open the donuts and bit into one, dusting white powder from her fingers before offering Jess the package. "Want some?"

"No. Those are all saturated fat."

"They taste wonderful. I burned breakfast, and I'm starving."

"You burned breakfast?"

"Yes. Set off the fire alarm and everything."

"You know, you could cook if you wanted to."

"Maybe. I probably could learn to tap dance too, if I wanted to."

"Not so sure about that, but I'd like to see you give it a shot." Jess grinned, and for a moment, she simply stared. It was good to see him smile at her instead of the usual frown of disapproval.

"I guess you're into cooking, then?" she commented.

"I'd have to eat donut gems if I wasn't."

Kate laughed. "Where do you live anyhow?"

"I rent a little house on Third Street. It's all I need right now. Plenty of room for me and the boys."

"The boys?" She raised a brow. "You have roommates?"

"Cats."

Kate blinked. "Cats?"

"Not macho enough for you?"

She grinned and raised her palm. "I didn't say that."

"Your eyes did." He shrugged. "And for the record, the cats are your brother's doing."

"What?" Kate nearly snorted at the words. "You too?"

"Yeah. Tucker is pretty persuasive."

"That's the truth." She smiled. "Tell me about your boys."

"They're bonded brothers. They keep each other company, and they keep me company too. I was skeptical at first. Also a little annoyed that I fell for his sales pitch. Turns out, they're the best thing that's happened to me in a long time. It's an added perk that Olive likes to come over to play with them. I can't get more than a peep out of her most of the time."

"Olive is very shy, isn't she?"

"She used to be much more outgoing. Her father was her world, and when he left… I think Olive blames herself."

Kate nearly gasped, staggered by Jess's words. She'd make a point of finding a way to talk to Olive. Sadly, they had a lot of pain in common.

"Mind if I ask what the story is with Nicole?" Kate finally asked.

"Not much to tell. She married right out

of college. My father wanted her to go to med school. She got as far as taking the MCAT exams. Then she was terrified that she would pass. So she eloped before the results came in."

"Did she pass?"

"Oh, yeah. Of course she did. Got the results thirty-five days later. Two weeks after that, she found out she was pregnant with Olive."

"So what happened?"

"Not a thing. She worked until Olive was born. Her husband took off when Olive was six. He couldn't handle being tied down."

Kate sighed. "That does seem to happen. They should have classes in high school that deal with adulting."

"Remember in high school when we had to go home with those baby dolls to get a glimpse of being a parent?" he asked.

"Infant simulator." Kate shook her head. "I'll never forget that project. It cried half the night I took the doll home. Every time I changed position, that baby wailed. I fed it, changed the diaper, burped it and rocked the thing. It only cried louder. Finally, Mitch felt sorry for me and took it so I could get a few hours of sleep. I ended up with bonus points."

"You cheated."

"*Cheated* is such a strong word. The point is that I got the moral of the story. I don't have any kids, do I?"

Jess chuckled. "Does that mean you don't ever want kids?"

"I love kids. I love spoiling them and then returning them to their owners. However, I'm probably not a good candidate for full-time parenting." Kate glanced at Jess, then looked away. He'd be a great father. Yes, Jess McNally was a rules guy, and he was patient and slow to anger. She'd be a terrible role model for children with her rebel ways. The thought brought a wave of unexpected pain as memories of her parents and the big brothers who raised her filled her mind. She blinked back emotion and crumpled the napkin on her lap.

"You okay?" he asked.

"I'm fine."

"Why does your face look like you want to ask me something?"

"Does your mother know?" The words burst from her lips before she could consider the wisdom of the question.

"Know what?"

"That you… That you proposed."

"No," he murmured without looking at her.

Kate nodded, processing the answer. There was no satisfaction in knowing she'd only hurt one McNally. She stood and dusted off her hands. "We better get back."

"Right." Jess stood, as well. "Thanks again."

"Sure. Anytime. I don't work weekends right now. I guess I will once the cast is off and I transition to the stables full time. So if you need help with your mom, use me."

"That's pretty generous of you."

"Your mom is a wonderful person, and she's a link to my mother. I feel a connection to her. Whatever I can do to help, I will."

"Thanks, Kate. You know, I can tell my mother feels the same way about you."

"That still worry you?" she asked.

Jess cringed. "I deserved that, didn't I?"

She shrugged. Would he ever be able to trust her?

"I'm really sorry," Jess said. "My only defense is that she's the only parent I have left."

"I get that." She turned to go. "Maybe now you can understand why it was so important for me to find my father."

Kate got in her truck, pulled out the brochure from Susan's nurse and read every page front to back for the third time that day. She dug in her purse for her cell and called Dr. Bowie's office at the Rebel Clinic.

"Hi. I'd like to schedule a visit with Dr. Bowie. Yes. I know I have an appointment for my X-ray. This is for something different. I want to talk with her about a few things. Sure. I can hold. Thank you."

Music echoed in Kate's ear as she waited. She stared at the brochure, turning it over once again. Could this be the reason she was back in Rebel?

Chapter Seven

"Uncle Jess, are we really going to give Miss Kate a cooking lesson?" Olive asked. She glanced at Kate's house and then looked at him.

"It was your idea, O favorite niece." He yawned before smiling down at the sweet girl at his side.

"You don't have any other nieces, Uncle Jess."

"That too."

Olive giggled as she followed him up the walk to the door. He rang the bell and stepped back, waiting for Kate to answer, fighting off another yawn.

Jess had lain awake last night, unable to

sleep. He kept seeing his mother in that hospital bed, so pale, her arms hooked up to the IVs and her dialysis graft site visible in the hospital gown. Hospitals scared him. He was a guy who liked to be in control, and he had no control over anything once he walked through those glass doors and down those antiseptic-scented halls.

His mother had been hospitalized only a few times since her diagnosis, and each time, he'd felt helpless. While he knew that the cell phone issue yesterday had not been his fault, guilt gnawed at him because he'd let his mother down.

Seeing Kate at his mom's bedside had been a powerful wake-up call that he needed to accept help when it was offered. It didn't escape him that he'd preached the same sermon to Kate.

He was more than grateful for Kate's quick willingness to step in. According to his sister, Kate had done so without even being asked. She'd been a real friend to their family, which made him regret how he'd jumped to conclusions at his mother's house. Yeah, yesterday had been a turning point. He'd apologized to Kate. Now he wanted to prove he meant it.

"I don't think she's home, Uncle Jess."

Shifting the box in his arms, he knuckled a tune on the door. "Yeah, she is. I called her after church and told her I would drop something off, and she said she'd be here." Jess nodded to the rust bucket in the drive. "Her truck is here."

A loud clang sounded from the backyard, followed by a shout of exasperation.

"That sounds like Miss Kate," Jess said.

They followed the path around the garage to the gate and into the yard, where Kate sat on the thick grass in jeans and an orange-and-black Oklahoma State University T-shirt. She was surrounded by a long cardboard box and various lengths of metal pipes, all spread around her. When she saw his niece, she grinned. "Hi, Olive."

Olive offered a shy wave of hello.

"Nice yard," Jess said. His gaze spanned the cozy expanse of green lawn shaded by the lazy branches of a tall magnolia.

A breeze tickled the chimes on the back porch, and they sang a soft melody.

"Thanks. Tucker did everything. I'm the groundskeeper du jour."

"And an excellent one." He frowned at the disarray around her. "What are you doing?"

"Isn't that obvious?"

"Not really."

"I'm putting a hammock together. It'll be perfect beneath those trees over there, in the shade." She sighed. "Me, a good book, a tall tea and a hammock."

"That's very ambitious. However, I'm not sure you're going to get this done with a cast on your arm that stretches to your thumb."

"The lack of two hands is not the issue. It's the instructions." She tossed the white booklet onto the ground. "Unfortunately, they're written in Klingon. I took Spanish in college. Silly me."

Jess laughed. "I can see how that might be problematic. Perhaps I can be of assistance."

She perked up at his words. "You know Klingon?"

"Fluent. But first, I need to get the groceries into your house."

"Groceries?" Her blue eyes widened, and she gave him an adorably confused smile. "You brought me groceries?"

"Olive and I are here to give you a cooking lesson."

"What?" Kate scrambled to her feet, her gaze shifting to Olive. "A cooking lesson? Really?"

Olive nodded hesitantly. "Because you said you can't cook."

"I did admit that, didn't I?" Kate turned to him again. "You said you were going to stop by and drop something off."

"I am." He nodded. "I'm dropping off Olive and myself and a few groceries."

"Someone might have bent the truth," Kate murmured in a singsong voice.

"Nope. It's all about your interpretation."

"Right." She gave a slow shake of her head. "What's in the box?"

He turned to hide the carton from her inspection. "We'll get to that."

"Grandma says to tell you thank you for staying with her at the hospital," Olive said.

Kate brushed the grass off her jeans. "Is she home already?"

"Yeah," Jess said. "Doing well. She had a touch of the flu, and the associated side effects threw off her electrolytes. We now have a plan in place for sick days." His mother was his responsibility, and he wouldn't have a repeat of what had happened yesterday. Once again, he'd let everyone down, and in front of Kate too.

"Wonderful," Kate said. Again, she looked between them. "I'm sorry to repeat myself, but you two are really here to give me a cooking lesson?"

"Uh-huh," Olive said. "Mom and I made copies of our favorite recipes too."

"Olive doesn't want you to eat cereal every day, and she suggested we teach you how to fish."

Kate straightened and put a hand on her hip in mock offense. "I know how to fish. I once caught a forty-pound channel catfish in Lake Tenkiller."

"Don't be literal," Jess said. "Olive has been quite concerned."

"Oh, Olive. You are so sweet." Kate smiled at his niece. "What are we making?"

"Grandma's stew in the slow cooker," Olive said. "Because you said you like it." Jess grinned at her decisive words.

"That sure was yummy. But I don't have a slow cooker."

Olive's lips twitched, and her eyes lit up. "Yes, you do. We bought you one."

Jess held up the box, this time allowing her to see the picture on the side. "Here you go. Top-of-the-line slow cooker."

"Ooh! Very pretty. I don't think I have ever seen one of these up close."

"You will today," Jess said. "We'll get your dinner going, and then we can put the hammock together."

Kate leaned close to him. "For clarification, you spent your hard-earned money on a pot that's only purpose is making stew?" She paused. "What do I do with it the rest of the time?"

"You can make lots of things in the slow cooker, and you can't mess it up," he said.

Kate laughed. "And here I thought you knew me."

Jess shook his head at her self-deprecating remark. She was poking fun at herself as usual. "You'll see," he murmured.

Once the groceries were unpacked, Jess pulled a cookbook out of another bag. "This is what we lay chefs call a cookbook. This one is specifically for slow-cooker meals. Soon you'll be hosting dinner parties, thanks to Olive and me."

Kate laughed again, and the sound warmed him. "I love your fearless optimism. It's an admirable trait." She thumbed through the pages, pausing to glance at the glossy pictures. "These meals look amazing." She closed the book. "I probably shouldn't get my hopes up, though. Or yours."

"Don't tell Olive that."

"No pressure, Jess. I have to get this right or crush a little girl's heart? Is that what you're saying?"

"No, this is bigger than that." He peeked out the door to the living room where Olive and Bella both watched a squirrel out the window. "She wants to learn to ride, and she's working up the courage to ask you."

"Why don't you take her?"

"She idolizes you. Olive is a reader and a horse lover. She's already checked out all the horse novels from the library, so Nicole has had to start ordering them online. I mentioned your rodeo background to Olive, and that was it. I've become the second string. Benched for the duration. You're her hero."

Jess started to say more and clamped his jaw shut. How could he explain how vulnerable Olive was without offending Kate again? He could only pray she understood how much responsibility lay in being a hero in the eyes of a shy little girl who'd been abandoned by someone she loved.

Instead of her usual witty response, Kate was silent as she seemed to consider his words. Finally, she picked up the slow cooker's instruction book and turned to the table of contents. "I don't know about this. I'm concerned it's another opportunity for me to feel bad about my lack of skill in this particular area and disappoint a ten-year-old at the same time."

"I'm telling you, Kate—" he patted the glass cover on the stainless steel pot "—this baby is foolproof."

"You keep saying that, Jess, but I beg to differ. When it comes to me and cooking, failure is the only option."

"No. I mean it. There are three steps. Put the food in. Set the timer to the desired time. Eat."

Kate dropped her head and sighed. "You missed one. Turn off the smoke detector."

"Nope, won't happen. If you set it for, say, eight hours, it goes to warm mode when it hits eight hours. You really cannot mess this up."

"Promises, promises." She chuckled. "I should show you my last attempt at becoming a culinary queen."

"Your last attempt?"

She pulled the toaster from the pantry. "My toaster is…toast. Pun intended."

Jess assessed the black scorch marks on the top of the appliance and shook his head. "Slow cookers trump toasters. Not even in the same league." He stepped to the doorway. "Olive, we're ready to start. Ask Bella if she wants to wash the mushrooms."

"Uncle Jess," his niece groaned.

"Oops, I keep forgetting. No opposable thumbs. You'll have to help her."

Twenty minutes later, Kate wiped down the counter while constantly shooting glances at the slow cooker. "Who knew it was this easy? You're sure we don't have to peel those potatoes?"

"Wash and quarter. That's it." Jess gave a thumbs-up.

"I'm amazed. Amazed."

"How about if we put the hammock together?" he asked.

"Sure. You go ahead. I want to show Olive something."

"Okay, I can do that." Jess stepped outside through the patio door and picked up the instruction booklet from the lawn. He took two steps toward the front yard and his truck and stopped. He'd left his tool-box in the stables earlier in the day. Surely, Kate had a screwdriver.

When he walked back into the house, Kate and Olive were in the living room examining Kate's spun-glass horse collection, their dark heads together.

"Where did you get these?" his niece asked. Reverence laced her voice.

"I've collected them from different cities where I've visited rodeo events." Kate picked up the amber glass stallion with a blue mane and held it up to the light. "This was my very first one. My father gave it to me."

When Olive was silent for a beat, Jess struggled not to interrupt the moment. He regretted eavesdropping yet was unable to move.

"My daddy left," Olive whispered. "It's my fault."

Even across the room, Jess could feel the pain in his niece's voice, and a heavy weight slammed into him.

Kate stooped down until she was eye level with Olive. "No. Don't ever say that. Ever. It's not your fault."

Olive shook her head. "It is, Miss Kate. I got in trouble, and the next day, he was gone."

"It doesn't have anything to do with you, Olive. Your daddy loves you, even if he can't show you."

"Then why did he go away?"

"My daddy left too. I know that it's hard to understand, but we have to remember that their leaving doesn't mean they don't love us."

Jess swallowed as Kate continued.

"Maybe you and I will never know why they left, but it still doesn't mean they don't love us. Leaving is all about them. Only them. Do you understand?"

Olive gave a slow nod.

When Kate picked up the horse her father had given her and offered it to Olive, Jess caught his breath.

"I want you to have this. Put it someplace safe where you can see it and remember that God loves you so much that He counts the hairs on your head." She touched Olive's dark tresses and offered a small smile. "Imagine that. You are loved so much by your heavenly Father, that He knows the number of hairs on your head. And His love for you never changes."

Jess's heart nearly exploded at the exchange, his own emotions threatening to take over. He tried to slip back out the door undetected, but Kate's gaze met his, and he froze.

"I, um, I need a screwdriver."

"Oh, is that all? Here I thought you were going to tell me you couldn't read Klingon after all." She stood and led the way to the kitchen.

"Am I imagining things, or can I smell that stew already?" Kate asked, her voice unnaturally bright, though she wouldn't look him in the eye.

"You are definitely not imagining things," he said.

When she handed him the screwdriver, he put his hand over hers. "Thank you."

She lowered her eyes. "I didn't do anything."

"Yeah, you did."

When she finally looked up at him, her blue eyes were moist and raw with pain. She licked her lips and released a breath. "No little girl should ever go through her life believing that sort of lie, Jess."

Without thinking, Jess tucked her to his side and held her close. The scent of mango and regret filled his senses. He sighed and released a breath. "I know, Kate. I know."

Kate checked the slow cooker. She couldn't believe how one ceramic pot had revolutionized her life. Beef stew Sunday thanks to Olive, and today, she had chicken and rice cooking. If all went well, she might very well invite Olive and Jess back for dinner.

After filling Bella's water fountain and giving her breakfast, she walked up the road past the admin building and to the stables. The first influx of official summer guests had checked in, and though

Kate wasn't supposed to actually touch the horses, Jess had eased his restrictions as long as she didn't ride. They'd compromised, which was another step forward. In return, Kate utilized the two college-aged girls she'd hired. Hired herself, without the assistance of Jess or her brothers and trained them both to be able to discern the greenhorns from the skilled riders. They knew the safety protocols and were ready to begin teaching.

As she approached the stable entrance, she saw Reece coming around the corner, tugging leather gloves from his hands. A smile lit up his face when he saw her. "Hey, little sister. How's everything going?"

"Really good."

"That's what we want to hear." Reece looked at her, a question on his face. "Mitch suggested that you might be avoiding us, but I didn't believe that for one minute."

"I saw you at the Monday staff meeting."

"But you skipped Sunday dinner last week, so he thinks you've got something on your mind you aren't sharing."

Leave it to Mitch to figure out when she was spending a lot of time in her head. Thinking and praying about the realities of donating a kidney had occupied most of her thoughts of late. But she wasn't ready to share with her family until the doctor gave her the okay, and she was firm about her decision.

"I'm fine, Reece. Really."

"That Mitch is a troublemaker." Reece grinned. "Refresh my memory. The cast is coming off soon, right?"

"Correct. After Memorial Day."

"Hey! Good news. Congratulations." He offered a high five.

"Thanks. I'll be gone for an hour to the clinic for the removal ceremony."

"No problem. As I recall, you took a day off this past week for medical tests. Everything okay?"

Kate eyed him. Had someone told him about the appointment for testing as a potential kidney donor? "How did you know that?" she asked.

"I'm the boss. I sign off on everything."

"Right. I had some lab work. Nothing to do with the arm."

"If you say so. Just so you're healthy."

"Very healthy." Another doctor appointment, and she hoped to be past the first hurdle toward becoming a donor candidate.

"Once you have a medical release, turn it in to Violet," Reece said. "Oh, and the new ranch T-shirts came in. Violet has them at her desk. We like the staff to be easily identified."

"*Staff.*" She savored the word. "I'm so excited to be an official staff member."

"Are you messing with me?" he asked. "Because I never thought I'd see the day you'd be excited about a T-shirt or Rebel Ranch."

"I'm becoming a part of all this, and I like it." Even as she said the words, it sank in how very true they were. Something had changed when she wasn't looking.

"You do? In truth, I wasn't even sure you'd last this long."

Kate jerked back at the admission. "So little confidence in your sister?"

"Total confidence. But I understand the call of the circuit."

Kate cocked her head and stared at her brother. To be fair, both Reece and Mitch had given her a wide berth since she'd arrived, allowing her to make her own decision about the future. "You expected me to leave?"

"I said I understand the pull of the rodeo. Your presence here is a gift for however long you're able to stay."

"Thank you, Reece."

"I'll see you at the hoedown next Friday?"

"Absolutely," Kate said.

"And you're going to the family get-together at Tucker's house on Saturday?"

"Saturday?"

"Yeah, you know. Memorial Day weekend?"

"Um, no. I mean, we've had family time nearly every weekend since I arrived. I made other plans."

"Plans. Okay. Plans are great. Good for you." He looked her over. "You're sure everything is okay, Kate?"

"It is. Don't worry about me. I'm doing fine."

"Yeah, that's exactly when I do worry about you." He met her gaze with his usual Reece-furrowed brow. "You know where to find me if you need anything."

"I do. Now, go be the boss."

She left her brother and walked up to the pen where Giddy and Gabby, the docile new paint horses from Plume, stood patiently as the training staff demonstrated equine etiquette to guests. Kate itched to ride the pair. As soon as she was cleared, she planned to ride Einstein and then every single horse in the guest stable one by one.

"Everything okay?"

Kate whirled around at Jess's voice.

"Yes. Do I look sick or something? You're the second person to ask me that."

Jess raised his palms. "Easy there. You were staring out into space. It was merely a question. Not an accusation."

"I was daydreaming about the time I'll be able to ride again."

"Ah. Makes perfect sense." He nodded. "How's your balance therapy going?"

"One more session."

"You're feeling good? No further episodes?"

"Not a one. I have a follow-up appointment with Uncle Bobby coming up. I don't want to get ahead of myself, but…" She paused and then grinned. "Who am I kidding? I'm miles ahead of myself, and I fully expect to be cleared."

"That's great, Kate."

"It's progress. Toward what, I'm not sure. But it's progress."

"How's everything going at the guest stable? Need any help?"

"No. We're set. Joy is training the adults, and Cindy is handling the youth. Every ride slot from now through the Memorial Day holiday is filled."

"That's great." He paused. "Did Nicole call to schedule Olive?"

Kate nodded. "Yes. We decided to start next Saturday. So she could be here to watch."

"Thanks for doing that."

"My pleasure." She grinned and glanced around, excitement bubbling. "This is fun, isn't it? Being part of launching a new season."

"Yeah. It is. I really like being part of the big picture."

"Yes. That's what it is. This is the first time I've felt like I'm contributing, and it's gratifying." It was gratifying and gave her a glimpse of what it would be like to stay here long-term. Was she ready to put down roots, or was Franny's job offer enough to lure her back on the road? She wasn't sure.

"I'll tell you something you're going to like even more," Jess said. "Being part of this means you get to eat in the mess hall. Did you see the menu Chef Luna has posted for the kick-off? It starts right after the hoedown."

"No, I didn't. I've been pretty focused on my slow cooker. I haven't eaten in the mess hall since before Olive's cooking lesson."

"Is that right?" Jess chuckled. "Well, this menu will make you put the slow cooker away, at least for now. Check it out. It's on the corkboard in the admin building near the coffee machine."

"Couldn't you just tell me?" she asked.

"Nope. But I plan to eat at the ranch mess hall every single night that week."

Kate stared at him. Was that an invitation? No. She was surely reading too much into the statement. The cooking lesson with his niece had marked a change in their relationship. They were getting along. She was willing to overlook his defection to her brothers for now, and perhaps he was beginning to trust her motives. Tentative friends. That was a good place to be.

His phone buzzed, and he pulled it out of his pocket. "I better run. There's a photography session going on at the gazebo. I'm headed there to assist the photographer and ensure the ranch remains intact."

"Intact?"

"The couple have requested cattle in the picture."

"What? How are you going to do that? The liability alone is an issue."

"Not if Willard brings Baby up there. I figure I better be on hand in case she decides to be difficult."

"Baby's a dairy cow. How are you substituting a dairy cow for cattle?"

"The bride and groom are social media celebrities from Los Angeles. They won't know the difference. As long as they can get some pictures for social media, they'll be happy. They've already scheduled a blow-out wedding reception at the ranch event building at the end of the summer. Big bucks."

"I've never quite understood all the fuss and the money people spend on weddings."

His gaze met hers, and she saw a flash of something in his eyes. Kate knew what he was thinking. Ten years ago, she could have been getting married. To him. She quickly clamped her mouth shut.

Jess cleared his throat and nodded toward the UTV. "I guess that means I can't tempt you to come along to check out the photo shoot?"

"I regret that I must decline. Though

it sounds like fun." She rolled her eyes. "Not."

When he smiled, she was relieved they had moved past the awkward moment.

"We're still on for the rodeo?" Jess asked.

"Yes."

"I'm looking forward to it."

She nodded as he got into the UTV. Oddly, she was looking forward to attending the Decker rodeo with Jess, as well. This would be the first time he would have a glimpse of her in her world. Sure, he'd come to her competitions when she was in college. This was different.

Why it mattered, she didn't know.

Kate sensed Jess had begun to understand her in a new way. That worried her. She feared she might easily give him a piece of her heart again. Another thing to add to her thinking time. Thinking time was the long hours spent on the back porch glider and in her hammock contemplating kidney donations, Rebel Ranch, family...and Jess.

Chapter Eight

~ ❧ ~

"Looks like a good-sized crowd." Jess glanced around. "Great weather for an out-door-arena rodeo."

Overhead, a brilliant blue sky provided a bright backdrop for the event. The ride to Decker had been pleasant, and he was glad he'd accepted Kate's invitation. Now he followed her up to the ticket box, decorated with star-spangled bunting. The young girls selling tickets wore red, white and blue Western shirts and white cowboy hats.

"I guess I should have worn a flag or something," he said.

Kate laughed. "Rodeo folk love red, white and blue holidays."

"I forgot about the enthusiasm level in Oklahoma."

She grinned and handed him a twenty-dollar bill. "Here you go."

"Put your money away," Jess said. "Gents don't let ladies pay."

"If you pay for my ticket, this might be construed as a date."

"Yeah, we wouldn't want that, would we?" Jess found himself momentarily annoyed. Was he letting himself get caught up in their history? He brushed the emotion off, passed a bill to the girl in the booth and held up two fingers. Today, he was determined to enjoy the friendship he and Kate had sowed and not delve too deeply into anything else.

"Fine. You buy the tickets," Kate said. "I'll buy the popcorn. A big bucket. I'm hungry."

"Sounds good."

Kate had dressed in full cowgirl, and he couldn't help but appreciate the white Western shirt and red boots. A shiny gold buckle from her barrel racing days decorated her snug Levi's. Yeah, the cowgirl looked fine, and she seemed completely oblivious to the second glances from those around her.

Instead, she eyed the crowd, her gaze intent as they continued to walk.

"What are you looking for?" Jess asked. "Do you know someone here?"

"Entirely possible," she murmured.

At her words, the penny fell through the slot. "You're looking for your dad, aren't you?"

"I guess so." Kate met his gaze before she looked away with a shrug. "After ten years, it's become a habit."

"You've never seen him?"

"No, TJ Rainbolt is like vapor. I've searched online, and I've talked to my share of old-timers. Occasionally, someone will think they remember the name. It usually turns out that they're remembering Reece from when he used to bull ride."

"Reece ever run into him?"

"I never specifically asked. I guess I assumed he would have said something."

For the first time, Kate's journey, her search for her wayward father, really hit him and became real. He scanned the crowd filling the arena too, his heart growing heavy as he imagined her pain. He'd lost his father quickly due to a heart attack. He couldn't imagine living his life without knowing what happened to a loved one.

"I'm sorry, Kate."

She gave an adamant shake of her head. "No. I won't have you feeling sorry for me. You never did when we were younger, so don't start now. I can't look at you and see pity in your eyes, Jess. Nothing good can come of that."

The set of her jaw and the frown on her face said Kate was annoyed. He'd hit a hot button for sure. Though she sped up, her long legs were no match for him. He put a hand on her arm.

"Kate, empathy is not pity."

"Is that what your father had? Empathy?"

"My father?"

"Your father used to pity me, until you and I became friends. That's when his pity turned to hate. Why do you suppose he hated me so much?"

Jess's head jerked back at the words. "My father didn't hate you. He thought being poor was contagious." Saying the words out loud for the first time was uncomfortable. Admitting to the obvious flaw in Jacob McNally made Jess feel complicit for not calling him out years ago.

"Are you serious?" Kate said and kept walking. Her pace picked up again, as though she were running from something.

"Sadly, yes. My grandfather was a dirt-poor farmer. Dad scraped his way through college and then on to medical school."

Kate released a frustrated breath. "Shouldn't that have made him compassionate?"

"It made him afraid. Afraid that he was one bank deposit away from his past."

"That's terrible, but it sure explains a lot."

As he stared at her, an ominous tightness filled his chest. "What do you mean?" he murmured.

"Your father warned me away from you."

Jess froze, eyes fixed on Kate while people streamed around them. "My father did what?"

"We're blocking traffic." She took his arm and pulled him to a secluded spot near a fire exit. "Your father told me I wasn't good enough for you, and that I should back off."

He could only continue to stare, unable to complete a sentence as he worked to process her words. It was one thing for him and his dad to disagree, but he was stunned and disappointed that his father had reached out to Kate.

Kate kicked at a stone on the ground with the tip of her boot. "I can't believe we're talking about this now. Here."

"Is that why you left?" He asked the question that had haunted him for ten years.

"I was always going to leave. I told you that. You didn't listen. Your father's disapproval… Maybe it helped me to justify walking away."

"He was wrong, Kate." The words burst from his lips as their impact barreled straight into his gut. Could he have prevented Kate from leaving? Did it matter anymore?

She stared at him, eyes round.

"You know that, right?" he persisted.

"I'm not sure what I know, Jess."

"Kate Rainbolt," a deep voice called. "Where have you been, young lady?"

Kate and Jess turned to find a silver-haired gentleman with a black cane strolling toward them. He wore a black hat, a Western suitcoat with fancy stitching on the yoke and crisply creased Levi's.

"Petey!" Kate gasped with surprise and moved to offer the old cowboy a hug.

She turned to Jess. "Pete Miller, this is my friend Jess McNally."

"Pleased to meet you, son."

"You as well, sir."

"Pete was my instructor at clown school."

"And she's one of the best." Pete narrowed his eyes. "I heard what happened. Spoke to Beau. How're you holding up?"

"I'm much better."

Pete's gaze held a warm affection as he

nodded, slowly assessing. "Word spreads fast, Kate. Everyone on the circuit is proud of you."

"Thanks, Pete. That means a lot."

"Are you coming back?"

"I don't know." Kate's eyes flicked to Jess, and an unspoken communication passed between them. She knew she was bending the truth. There was no way Kate Rainbolt should be in that arena in this lifetime.

Pete pulled a card from his pocket. "Keep me posted. If you don't want to bullfight, I might be able to find a place for you at the school."

Jess observed the exchange with concern. He wanted the best for Kate, everyone did, but it was difficult to see her face light up because of an offer that might end up luring her away from home again.

"Your friend Pete looks like a river-boat captain, not a rodeo clown," Jess observed as the gentleman strolled away.

A musing smile touched Kate's mouth. "You're right. He's an actor once the greasepaint goes on. One of the best." She glanced toward the arena. "We better catch some seats."

Once they'd settled, Kate turned to him. "Being here for the first time since the accident is a little surreal. That's the only defense I have for slamming you with stuff you didn't need to hear."

"I did need to hear it." She'd answered questions that had kept him awake many a night until he'd made the decision to put Kate Rainbolt behind him. As for his father... Well, it seemed that he was overdue for a conversation with his mother about that.

"Excuse us."

Jess stood to allow two young girls to move to the empty seats farther down the row. As they passed, the scent of buttered popcorn teased, and Kate turned to him with an alarmed look on her face.

"What's wrong?" he asked.

"I didn't get the popcorn."

Jess grinned. "We'll get some later."

Overhead, the microphone popped and

screeched before the announcer began the opening-ceremony chatter. The crowd roared as a team of four flagbearers with red-white-and-blue-fringed chaps, holding American flags, thundered into the arena, their white horses kicking up dust. They raced across the arena in a figure-eight pattern before stopping in the middle, each one facing a section of the grandstands as the national anthem began.

Jess and Kate stood with their hands over their hearts while the stirring lyrics of the patriotic song rang out. Applause followed, along with hoots, whistles and hollers.

"That song always gets me," Kate said. "There's something so American about rodeo."

"Maybe you should suggest a small rodeo on Rebel Ranch. You'd be the perfect person to launch that kind of project."

Kate's eyes lit up. "Do you think Reece would be open to the idea?"

"Why not? He's a rodeo guy."

Their conversation ended as the barrel racing began. A fan-favorite event, the crowd stomped their feet and clapped their hands along with the introductory music.

Event after event, Kate and Jess cheered and yelled along with the crowd. When the bull riding competition was announced, Kate tensed.

The announcer's voice pitched higher with excitement, and the crowd responded with cheers. "Now for the event you've all been waiting for. Bull riding."

Both Jess's and Kate's attention went to the chute. A cowboy stood with his boots on either side of the chute gate as he prepared to ease down onto the animal.

"Say a prayer for Jerome Callum, ladies and gents. This cowboy has drawn Despiadado."

Silence fell over the arena, followed by hushed murmurs. All eyes were on the cowboy.

Kate looked at the aisle and then put a hand on his sleeve. "I saw a gift shop when we drove through town. Let's go find Olive a glass horse."

"What?" He did a double take at the sudden request. "You don't want to stay for this?"

"No." She stood, ready to move past him. "Jess, I have to get out of here."

He looked up at the leaderboard and then back at Kate. Her face had paled, and beads of perspiration clung to her forehead. It took half a second to figure out what had spooked her.

Despiadado.

The same bull that had nearly killed her and a bull rider. Kate was having some sort of a post-traumatic-stress response right now.

He grabbed her arm before she stumbled and guided her to the aisle and away from their seats. Around them, the noise of the event became a roaring blur. "Easy there. Watch your footing." He took her hand. "Follow me."

Once they were outside the arena, Kate bent over, her free hand on her knee as she worked to collect herself.

A moment later, she stood and looked around. "Where are we?"

"I think I went out the wrong exit." He cocked his head to the left and led them past the stock pens to a food truck, where he bought her a lemon-lime soda.

"Thank you," Kate murmured. She pressed the cold can to her forehead. Though the color had returned to her face, her breathing remained shaky.

"Parking lot is real close. Let's get some air-conditioning going. Okay?"

"Yes, please."

For a few minutes, he let her sit quietly in the passenger seat, head back against the headrest, with her eyes closed as the cool air blew the dark strands away from her face. Finally, her lashes fluttered, and she looked at him. The bleak expression on her face nearly tore him apart.

"Don't I feel ridiculous?" she said softly.

"That bull almost killed you. I'd have the same reaction."

Kate gave a small nod of appreciation at his words. "It was like a movie," she said. "A loop, playing over and over in my head. I guess, up to now, I've been able to pretend that if I didn't think about it, it wasn't real." She took a shaky breath. "Suddenly, everything all came rushing back. The slow-motion tumble through the cool February air. Spitting out dirt as I bounced on the ground. I could hear the crack of my own ribs." She licked her lips, gaze straight ahead out the window. "Then a sharp burning pain."

"Oh, Kate." He grimaced at the emotion in her words.

"It's okay. I'll be fine." She rolled her hand into a fist and placed it against her mouth.

"Yeah, maybe if you tell yourself that enough times." He released a breath. "Kate, it's okay to show pain, and it's okay to allow others to share that pain."

When she turned to him, he realized that he'd leaned closer, nearly closing the distance between them in the cab. Kate moved toward him, near enough that he could feel the warmth of her breath against his chin.

Her lips parted, and for once, he didn't think, didn't breathe. Instead, he kissed her, gently slipping his hands through her silky, soft hair. He kept kissing until he was free-falling.

It was better than he remembered. The sweetness, the pull of his emotions as his heart slammed into his chest.

A fraction of a second later, he came to his senses and broke the contact. He moved away, placing his hands on the steering wheel as if to ground him. Or perhaps to keep himself from touching her, holding her and kissing her again.

"I, um…" He turned to Kate, fully expecting recriminations.

Kate reached up and covered his lips with her fingers, her blue eyes clear as they gazed into his. "Say nothing. Please, don't apologize. Don't. Just don't." She touched his hand on the steering wheel, and the contact was nearly his undoing.

A solemn silence stretched between them, and she returned her own hand to her lap and sat quietly.

Then she cleared her throat. "You know, I never did get that popcorn. I'm starving. Let's go find a Sonic and get some chili-cheese fries and a couple of cherry limeades."

"Food. Yeah, good idea." He put on his seat belt and started the truck.

Food might help him forget the touch of her lips, but would it help him forget that he was making a huge mistake by once again risking his heart with no guarantees?

Jess doubted it.

Kate grinned and said a silent prayer of thanksgiving as she left Rebel Clinic. She was a match for Susan. Not an exact match, but she had enough of the required antigens to move forward. Furthermore, her ultrasound showed very healthy kidneys with no irregularities. The next step would include a mental health exam and counseling. She had an appointment to visit with a donor in Tulsa for what the doctor called a reality check.

She would do whatever the physicians recommended, but as far as Kate was concerned, the Lord was her reality check. She'd spent nearly every evening since she'd visited Jess's mother in the hospital praying about this decision. The path was clear medically, and she was confident that she'd assessed the situation with her head and her heart. If only she had the same peace about the direction of her life.

Striding to her truck, Kate gave a firm nod. Today was the day to talk to Susan McNally.

It took circling the block twice before a parking spot opened up in downtown Rebel. Kate had to settle for one around the corner behind the Piggy Wiggly. She walked the block to Daisy's bakery and stared up at the lettering on the canvas awning. Daisy's Pies & Baked Goods was spelled out in gold lettering against a navy-blue background. Her sister-in-law Daisy provided the kind of success story she longed to emulate. Although today, Kate didn't appreciate the success as much. The line to the shop was out the door. Kate slowly inched forward for ten minutes until she was finally inside. Good thing she was in a spectacular mood.

The plan had been to arrive when the

bakery first opened, but getting out of bed had been an effort this morning after another restless night.

Who would be able to sleep well after a kiss like that from Jess on Saturday? She'd blathered on without a filter, and he'd responded by kissing her.

The rest of the holiday weekend, she'd been thinking about that kiss and doing something she'd avoided up until now. Thinking about the past. The what-ifs of her life.

She'd barely dated since leaving Rebel. She needed someone in her life that she couldn't run over. A man she could go toe-to-toe with, who respected and cherished her just the way she was. Was that man Jess?

Along with that question came the same fear. The fear that Jacob McNally was right. She wasn't good enough for his son. What would happen when Jess came to the same conclusion as his father?

Another customer left with a bag of pastries, and Kate stepped forward an inch. The bakery's glass cases were now in view, and she peeked around the bouffant hair of the woman in front of her to admire a row of pies with golden crusts.

"Kate!"

Kate's head jerked up, and she saw Daisy waving her to the front of the line. Kate obeyed, despite the glare of the woman in front of her.

"I called your name, like, three times. In your happy place?" Daisy linked her arm through Kate's.

"More like my overanalyze-my-life place."

"I've been there," Daisy said. "I do not recommend the extended-stay package."

Kate laughed, her mood immediately light again. Today was a day to rejoice. She would not allow herself to dwell on yesterday any further.

Daisy led her to a small room outside her office, where a table and chairs were set up along with a play yard and a bin full of toys. "Sit. Tell me what you need, and I'll grab it for you."

"This is a nice setup you have back here."

Her sister-in-law pushed back her red-gold

curls that had slipped from the baker's headscarf. "I bring the kids into work often, so I had to have a play area."

"What's going on out there?" Kate asked, thumbing in the direction of the front of the bakery. "Where did all those people come from?"

"That's the summer blessing. Aren't you ever here in the summer?"

"No. The circuit is pretty busy this time of year. Every small town west of the Mississippi, from here and into Canada, has a small-town summer tradition that usually includes an old-fashioned rodeo. That's rodeo-money time. Since the ranch opened five years ago, I try to be here for the hoedown weekend, but then I'm on the road again."

"You've missed the fun, then. Rebel Ranch has led the way for the economic explosion in Rebel. Reece's success was a wake-up call for the town. The local businesses banded together and successfully created a plan to lure the tourist trade. It started with a face-lift."

"I did notice how pretty downtown is," Kate said.

"All part of the plan. Out-of-towners drive down Main Street on their way to Rebel Lake and Keystone Lake, so shop owners decided to do their best to tempt them to stop. The strategy worked."

"What's the tourist population in the summer?" Kate asked.

"*The Weekly Rebel* reported that the transient summer tourist population headed to the lakes is around ten thousand."

"What? That's fantastic. I never realized. I mean, I knew it was busier here in the summer, but ten thousand is unbelievable."

"Which is why you should tell me what you need before my cases are empty."

"A cupcake, any flavor."

"Just one?"

"Yes. I'm celebrating good news with a friend."

"That's wonderful." Daisy smiled. "Any particular color frosting?"

"Purple is her favorite color."

"Purple it is. Be right back."

Minutes later, Daisy returned with a lavender-frosted cupcake in a white box gaily adorned with curls of purple-and-yellow ribbons.

"Oh, Daisy, this is perfect. What do I owe you?"

"Not a thing. We're family." She took the box and gently placed it inside a small yellow shopping bag with a daisy printed on the outside.

"Thank you, Daisy."

She leaned closer. "You look happy, Kate."

"Do I?" She smiled. "I guess I am."

"Any particular reason you want to share?"

"Summer in Oklahoma?" Kate offered.

"I'm thinking there's more to that sparkle in your eyes. Could it be a fella?"

"What?" Kate's jaw sagged.

Daisy gave a knowing nod. "Someone might have mentioned that you ditched us on Saturday for a date." She grinned and raised her brows. "Which I totally approve of."

"It wasn't a date," Kate sputtered. "And who told you that?"

"Stop by for dinner after church on Sunday and I might reveal my source. Oh, and the kids claim you owe them a Chutes and Ladders rematch."

"Rematch? They skunked me last time," Kate said.

When Kate finally walked out the door of the bakery, she was still smiling, but she was also determined to figure out what information the grapevine had shared.

Her interaction with Daisy had brought home the fact that she was blessed. She had more family than she could count on her fingers now. The idea of staying in Rebel had become more tempting, though it continually warred with her greatest fear. After ten years as a tumbleweed, could she put down roots forever?

Though Memorial Day was yesterday, the sidewalks of Rebel remained busy as Kate took off down Main Street. People peeked in storefronts and strolled along. Many vacationers enjoyed ice cream cones from a pop-up that had opened in the old movie theater next to the Jazzercise studio. At the intersection, Kate crossed to the other side of Main Street and headed toward the Saucy Potter. She'd already checked with Nicole and knew that Susan was working this morning.

Taking a breath, Kate said a silent prayer as she eased open the shop door.

"Kate. How nice to see you."

Kate looked up to find Susan offering a welcoming smile. Today, Jess's mother wore a purple paisley scarf with a white silk blouse. Somehow, she'd managed to make blue jeans elegant and dressed up.

"Hey, Susan. Have you got a minute?" Kate's gaze scanned the busy shop. "I'd like to chat. It won't take long."

"For you, I have many minutes. Let's go into the courtyard. Nicky hires a part-time cashier in the summer, so we're good unless she calls me."

Kate followed Susan outside to a secluded spot beneath a huge oak tree where a small outdoor table and chairs waited. The delicate tune of a wind chime tinkled as a soft breeze passed through. "This is so nice."

"It really is a little oasis, isn't it?" Susan smiled and reached for Kate's hand across the table. "Is everything all right, dear? This isn't about you and Jess, is it?"

"Me and Jess?" Heat rushed to her face. Surely, Jess hadn't mentioned that kiss?

"I was concerned the whole cooking lesson might have offended you."

"Oh, no. Actually, I'm grateful. Both he and Olive succeeded where others have failed. I throw things in that cooker and amazingly end up with dinner. I don't know who's more surprised, my cat or me. My smoke detector hasn't gone off once."

"That's wonderful. Maybe we can schedule our gingersnap lesson next."

My mother's gingersnaps. Kate's heart swelled. The words only affirmed her decision to proceed with the kidney donation. "Yes. Soon."

"To what may I attribute this visit?"

"I am here for celebratory reasons." Kate

placed the yellow bag on the table and withdrew the cupcake.

"You have my full attention now," Susan said.

The carefully worded speech she had practiced seemed less than adequate now that she faced Susan's anticipation. Kate hesitated for a moment. "I'm a match as a donor. Not a perfect match, but I've been cleared as a candidate."

Susan blinked. "A donor match. A kidney donor?"

Kate nodded.

"You?" Jess's mother released a small gasp and then stared at Kate, unblinking. "I didn't realize you were getting tested."

"Yes." Kate nodded. "The medical side is all clear. The final okay is pending a psychiatric evaluation."

"Kate. I don't know what to say. I never expected you to do this."

"I didn't want to tell you anything until I heard the results."

"I'm absolutely speechless." Susan wrung her hands together. "I guess that's why my doctor asked me to come in tomorrow." She shook her head in disbelief. "Are you sure you want to do this? Donating a kidney is... I don't know what to call it except for selfless. This is an absolute act of sacrifice."

"This is really not about me." Kate pushed back the emotion threatening to overflow. "I've prayed, and I have perfect peace about the decision. I know beyond a doubt this is what I am supposed to do. So please, don't think of it as something altruistic. I'm being obedient to a spiritual nudge."

Susan nodded slowly and was silent for minutes. "Please don't think I'm not appreciative. What I am is overwhelmed."

"That's okay. I know this is a surprise."

"Yes. That it is." She looked at Kate, her gaze searching. "You're very sure you want to do this?"

"I'm long past *if*. I'm at *when*."

"When? That's a scary question," Susan said.

"Not at all. Things are moving perfectly and in order."

"Do you have any idea when we'd proceed?" Susan shook her head. "I can't even believe I'm asking you that. I'd pushed the idea of a transplant out of my head. I didn't want to be disappointed." She sighed. "That's a terrible testimony, but there it is."

"I totally get that." Kate pulled out the calendar on her phone. "You'll need to chat with your physician. There are a lot of things to consider. I'm not a perfect match, which means more antirejection medication for you. But if you'd like to proceed, the general discussion is about early September."

"Oh, my. So soon." Susan stared straight ahead as though struggling to process the information. Then she turned back to Kate. "Does anyone else know?"

"No." Kate shook her head. "Susan, please don't tell Jess." She took a breath. "I should tell him myself. I also have to tell my brothers."

Susan cocked her head. "Your brothers may not be happy."

"That would factor in if I were six years

old. But I'll be thirty-one in the fall, and I've been on my own for ten years. I love and respect my brothers, but this isn't their decision." She cleared her throat. "I'll tell them after the hoedown. It's this Friday, and everyone is focused on that right now."

"That makes sense." She nodded. "Mum's the word."

"Yes, though you aren't obligated to proceed. You may decide you want to wait for a perfect match."

"I'll be praying of course." Susan leaned across the table and once again took Kate's hand. "Though right now, I'm feeling quite at peace myself."

Kate stood. She went to leave and then turned back. "May I ask you something? It's rather personal." It was very personal and had been chasing her thoughts since she and Jess were at the rodeo.

"Anything."

She licked her lips, working up courage. "Why didn't Jess's dad like me? Was it really because we were poor?"

"Oh, dear." Susan gestured with a hand. "You better sit down."

Kate slowly eased to the chair again.

"Your mother... Margaret and I were very close friends, as you know."

Susan was again silent as though measuring her words. "I was always aware that Margaret was the pretty one. She had no clue how beautiful she was, and that made her all the more attractive." She paused. "Jacob, my husband, was in love with her, but Margaret had eyes for only TJ.

"Eventually, Jacob got over it, and he and I began to see each other. Sometimes I wondered if I was playing second fiddle to your momma, but we had a good marriage, though he never forgave your mother for rejecting him. I do believe that's why he insisted I break off my relationship with her. And why he was horrified when you and Jess became close."

"I... I don't even know what to say," Kate returned. This wasn't the backstory she'd expected, and she found herself overwhelmed with mixed emotions.

"I'm sharing with you woman-to-woman, and I pray you keep that confidence. Jacob was a good man, a good father and a good doctor. But he wasn't perfect. He couldn't see what I could. That you are the woman that God put in Jess's life."

"Oh, I'm not sure that's something I can live up to."

"I don't want you to feel obligated, dear Kate."

That was a good thing, because once again, Susan had left her without a response. But for the first time since she'd left Rebel, she was able to let go of the words of Jacob McNally. There was a freedom that came with forgiving Jess's father. But was that freedom too late for her and Jess?

Chapter Nine

Jess looped his arms over the fence and pushed his straw cowboy hat to the back of his head. Around him, the scent of horse and Oklahoma dirt mingled with the sweet June sunshine as he observed the new mares in the pasture. As predicted, they were great with the inexperienced riders. Their good nature also made them a favorite for trail rides. Kate had named them Giddy and Gabby, which proved good for a few tongue twisters with the ranch guests.

"Jess, mind if I bounce a few ideas off you?"

He turned to find Dr. Finn Hardy at his side. "Sure. Keep in mind that I'm a couple of eggs short of a dozen right now. And what's left is scrambled. I spent the morning working on the June livestock budget."

"I hear you. I spent my morning with an old goat."

"An old goat?"

"Literally. Over at Ludlow Ranch. Stubborn fella, got his head stuck in a watering can."

Jess laughed. "Okay, you win. How can I help you, Doc?"

"It's about a woman."

Jess nearly groaned aloud. Instead, he held up a hand. "Wait right there. I am not the guy to be dispensing wisdom in that department. In fact, my advice might be hazardous to your health." And he sure did not want a play-by-play of the vet's love life either.

"Naw, I get that. Except you happen to be one of the few guys around here who is close to my age and single. Just hear me out."

Jess assessed Finn. He seemed like a solid guy. So what was the problem?

Finn ran a hand over his face and huffed a breath. "I thought you might have some insight. I want to ask a particular fair lady to the hoedown on Friday, but I don't know how to get out of the friend zone."

"Running late, aren't you? It's already Wednesday."

"Pure fear has kept me from approaching her sooner."

His curiosity now piqued, Jess crossed his arms and leaned his backside against the corral fence. "Fear? Has she turned you down before?"

"No. I haven't given her an opportunity."

"You're putting the cart before the horse. She can't say no or yes if you don't ask her, Doc."

"The thing is, I have a history of bad timing. I always seem to be attracted to women who are hung up on someone else."

"Who's she hung up on?"

"I haven't figured that out yet, which is what gives me half a hope that this time I might be wrong."

Jess cocked his head, his gaze on the vet.

"I'm having a hard time believing you have difficulty wrangling a date. From the chatter I hear, you're on the shopping list of every woman in Rebel."

Finn raised a hand in defense. "Through no fault of my own. I'm a congenial guy. My mama raised me that way." He shrugged. "Trouble is those lists belong to every sweet aunt and grandma in Rebel, and each of them has a family tree with a niece or granddaughter I should meet."

Jess blinked. "That's a problem?"

"It is when your affections are elsewhere occupied, as mine are."

"I say go for it. No guts, no glory, Finn." He shrugged. "Life's too short to worry about rejection."

Finn paused, staring out into the pasture. "Go for it, he says. Have I mentioned that this woman is way out of my league? One glimpse and...*whoosh*." He shook his head. "All I have to do is see her dark hair tumbling over her shoulders or hear her sweet laughter, and my gut nosedives. My tongue gets so tied, I can hardly get a word shoved out of my mouth the right way."

Dark hair? Jess frowned as Kate stepped out of the admin house and walked across the gravel toward the stable. She'd had her cast removed this morning and there was a bounce to her step that had been missing since her arrival at Rebel Ranch. It suddenly registered that he hadn't seen her much since Saturday. Had she been avoiding him since the rodeo? Jess sure hoped not, because despite the lack of wisdom of the action, he was certain that Kate had enjoyed the moment.

She turned in their direction and offered a cheery wave.

To him or Finn? They both returned her greeting.

Then it hit him. *Kate.* His heart thudded in his chest and his jaw dropped.

Surely, Finn didn't mean his Kate? Did he? Jess gave the vet a side-eyed evaluation. Willard was right, the guy was a woman magnet. So why was he concerned about a woman rejecting him?

Unless that woman was Kate? Even Jess had to admit that to the average observer, Kate Rainbolt was intimidating. He could understand Finn's reticence.

Kate was tall and sturdy and beautiful. The woman was whip-smart too. Book smart, street smart. It didn't escape him that with one arm in a cast, she had been managing Rebel's books and running the equine side of the ranch, and she hadn't dropped a single ball since she'd arrived.

Yeah, Kate could hold her own and more. Being raised by three brothers did that to you.

Jess glanced at Finn through new eyes. He didn't like the conclusion he'd tallied up. Not that he had any claim on Kate.

One kiss didn't mean anything except one kiss.

Though it had been a very good kiss.

He paused.

Did he want a claim on Kate? He wasn't sure anymore. The only thing clear was that he wasn't about to sit around and watch someone else set their sights on her without some resistance on his part.

"Ah, 'scuse me, Finn. I have to take care of something."

"Sure, man. Thanks for the talk."

Jess shoved off from the fence. "Yeah. Anytime. Hang in there. I'm sure this will work itself out."

"I hope it does before Friday night's hoedown."

Yeah, and so did Jess.

As predicted, Kate was in Einstein's stall, prepping for a ride.

"Congrats on the cast removal," he said. "You look happy."

"Understatement. I'm over the moon." She grinned but didn't face him, continuing to groom her best buddy.

"How's the arm? Two surgeries and months of being in a cast couldn't have been easy."

"The arm is a little puny, but the physical therapist gave me some exercises, and I'm noticing an improvement in the muscle tone already."

"So this is your first ride in how long?" He felt unable to stop rambling. Anything to keep up the conversation. The connection.

"Since the accident. The end of February."

"Yeah, I guess you're more than ready."

Kate nodded but said nothing further. When the silence stretched awkwardly between them, Jess glanced around to be sure they weren't overheard.

"Have you been avoiding me again?" he asked. "I'm guessing you're upset about that lapse of judgment at the rodeo."

"Is that what that was?"

"We work together. I'm the guy you report to. It's not exactly…"

"Not exactly what? We weren't at work." Kate leaned over, running assessing fingers over Einstein's legs, examining first one hoof and then another. "Either way, I'm not upset," she murmured.

"Are you mad about the cooking lesson? Did we insult you barging in like that?"

Kate laughed. "No. Not at all. Right

now, I have dinner simmering in that slow cooker."

"Whoa. I have to admit, I sort of thought you might be humoring us. You really are using it?"

"I am."

"So we're okay, then?"

"For the moment," she said.

For the moment was good.

"I'm a bit wound up is all," Kate continued. She rubbed Einstein's flank and reached for the saddle pad. "I could hardly sleep last night. I prayed all the way to the doctor's office this morning."

When she turned to pick up the saddle, Jess reached it first. Their hands collided, and Kate nearly jumped back at the contact.

"Um, sorry," she said. "I can handle this."

"I'd like to help you. That arm's got to be a little weak first day out of the cast. I'm guessing Einstein would appreciate my help, as well."

She sighed. "You're right. No use slapping leather on his back because my arm isn't up to the task. Thank you."

Once he'd put the saddle on the gelding, he turned to Kate. "Mind if I ride with you?"

"If you want to."

He was silent, overanalyzing her answer. "Maybe you want to be alone with Einstein. Quality time. I don't want to horn in."

"Jess, have you ever known me to be anything but forthright? If I wanted to ride alone, I would say so." She faced him. "I'd love to ride with you if you can stop hovering. And no back seat driving. I don't want to hear a word of critique or a single suggestion. I've been riding as long as I've been walking. You mind your horse, and I'll mind mine."

He grinned. "You drive a hard bargain, but it's a deal."

Kate walked Einstein out of the stable and waited in the sunshine. When he approached with his own mount, she glanced at him with hesitation.

"I'll need a boost," she eventually said. "I'm a little nervous about my arm."

"My pleasure." He waited for her to fasten her helmet and then offered his linked hands. It didn't escape him that weeks ago, she'd have used a mounting block rather than ask him for help. They'd come a long way in a short time.

"Thanks," Kate said as she sat victoriously astride the gelding. She looked around and smiled. "There was a time when I wondered if I'd ever be in the saddle again."

Jess mounted his mare and adjusted his hat to keep the full sun off his face. "How are you feeling about not being on the circuit? We're heading into summer. Isn't that the busiest time of the year in rodeo? This summer marks a new season for you."

"I've had to sit out before due to injuries, but it was always with the knowledge that I would be back in the saddle or the barrel, as the case may be." Kate lifted the reins. "I guess you're right. This time is different." She paused. "A new season? I like that. Perhaps that's the correct way to look at things. Along with thanking the Lord that I'm alive."

Kate leaned forward to stroke Einstein's mane. "I'm trying to think about this time as being a second chance to decide what I want to be when I grow up instead of looking at the situation as a limitation." She waved a hand in the air. "The options are endless. Except for being a chef. I've crossed that off my list."

"What about Pete's offer?" he asked.

"It's one of many options that I'm exploring."

"Many? Care to elaborate?"

"Franny asked me to be her assistant."

Jess frowned. He didn't like the sound of that. It was yet another option that would take her away from Rebel Ranch.

Kate looked at him. "What about you, Jess? When your mother gets well, are you going back to Montana?"

"I can't think that far ahead. There are so many obstacles to her health." He pointed toward the right. "Let's go over by the pond."

She nodded and directed Einstein toward the water. "You know," she said, "your mom just needs a donor."

He released a slow breath and met her gaze. "Let's not spoil your first ride. I don't want to talk about my mom's kidneys right now."

"Sure. Sure," she said.

"And you, Kate. Now that the cast is off, you are officially the equine manager." He eyed her quickly. Was it too much to hope that they'd reached a silent understanding, the rules of which were still a work in progress?

"Reporting to you. Are you asking if I mind that you're my boss?"

"Yeah, I guess I am. How are you feeling about that? Is it as distasteful as you thought it would be?"

"Not at all. I don't see you half as much as I feared." She laughed, her eyes sparkling with mirth. "I mean, as much as I thought I might."

Jess couldn't help but grin at her good humor. "Thanks a lot."

"It's the truth. I do the books and handle the horse situation. I'm in the admin building or the stables. You're out there on the ranch. I saw the records. You've nearly doubled the cattle since you've been here in Rebel and hired a few more wranglers to help. That's enough to keep you busy."

"And out of your hair?"

"I didn't say that."

"Are you attending the hoedown on Friday?" he asked.

"It's required. Aren't you?"

"Yeah. Sure. All the staff will be there and then some. Like Finn Hardy. He's not staff, but he'll be there." He paused. "Nice guy, that Finn."

Kate didn't respond to his bait. Instead, she slowed Einstein and nodded toward the rows of lazy weeping willows that guarded the pond. "Look through the branches at the sunlight on the water."

The Rebel pond was a misnomer. The pond was actually a stocked man-made lake for ranch guests. At this time of day, only a few guests sat on the pier, fishing. Ducks glided along the surface of the water, a few bobbing for lunch. The dappled sunshine on the lake was a prism of color shooting fractions of light onto the trees.

Jess turned to her, and she smiled. Together they slowly made their way around the pond, enjoying nature. Somehow they'd managed to return to their easy friendship of years ago, and he was grateful. For now it was enough.

He'd worry about Finn Hardy later.

"Where's your date?"

Kate whirled around at the sound of Jess's voice. "My what?" She nearly spewed her sweet tea. That was the last question she'd expected to come from the mouth of this particular cowboy. He had joined her at the back of the entertainment tent and stood close so she could hear him above the noise.

"Where's your date to the hoedown?" He glanced around with a frown.

"Have you been sniffing the enchiladas?" Kate cocked her head and assessed him, which was a very bad idea. All cleaned up and wearing a long-sleeved black Western shirt and crisp jeans, he was a very fine eyeful.

Jess laughed. "No. I thought Finn escorted you tonight."

"Finn Hardy?" Kate looked around the crowd in search of the tall, good-looking vet. "Our Finn? What are you talking about, McNally?"

Jess took off his hat and scratched his head. "You know, we're both well-educated people. Conversation shouldn't be this difficult."

This time, it was Kate who laughed. "Maybe we should try a simpler topic."

"Okay, you first."

"Is it my imagination, or is Saylor Tuttle channeling Dolly Parton?" Kate asked. "I've come home for a wedding three years running, and every year, her hair gets a little bigger."

"She's the pastor's wife, so I think it's

understood that the bigger the hair, the closer to—"

"That only counts in Texas," Kate interjected.

"Saylor is from Texas."

Kate opened her mouth to respond, but the music started up with a fiddle solo, which had them both paying attention.

"Who's the band?" Jess asked. He stepped around a few people to get a glimpse. "They sure sound familiar. Isn't that an L.C. Kestner song? If I close my eyes, I might think the band was here in Rebel."

"You've got a good ear." She grinned. "That is *the* L.C. Kestner."

"You're kidding, right? How did the ranch snag them?"

"Reece has friends in high places. Low places too," she said with a chuckle. "L.C. is an Okie."

"I'd heard that. She's from Tishomingo, right?"

"That's right. Reece used to work for her daddy in his previous career. L.C. and her band come here in the off-season to rest. My brother provides all the anonymity they need."

"How about that?" Jess stared as the fiddler flawlessly moved from a deep tone to a high-pitched note. Folks nodded and tapped their feet to the catchy tune as the music sparked smiles of enjoyment.

"Reece didn't tell anyone L.C. was playing tonight, and she's only doing one set. So it's a real treat, all the way around."

When the fiddler finished and applause filled the room, the band transitioned to a slow oldie. Overhead, the lights dimmed, and twinkling strings of curtain lights lent an intimate, dreamy atmosphere to the tent. Jess nodded toward the portable dance floor that awaited. "Would you like to dance?"

"I haven't danced in so long," Kate said with a nervous chuckle. "I think the last time was one of those square-dance fundraisers that the FFA held on Friday nights."

"Future Farmers of America. There's a

trip down memory lane." He took her hand. "Come on, before the song ends."

The scent of sandalwood and juniper drifted to her as she settled a hand on his shoulder. "You smell good." Kate nearly stumbled when she realized that her mouth had engaged without her. She could have kicked herself.

"Ah, thanks," he said.

An awkwardness settled between them, and for minutes, they both concentrated on the dance. When she missed a step and then recovered, their eyes connected. Humor lit up Jess's gray eyes.

"So, do you come here often?" he asked.

"What?" When his words registered, Kate laughed and found herself finally relaxing in his arms. "If you ask me my horoscope, I'm going to lose it," she returned.

He offered a lopsided grin. "Ever had that happen to you?" he asked.

"Worse. Oh, the lame pickup lines I could tell you about."

"I'd have thought rodeo cowboys were smooth," he said.

Kate shook her head. "Oh, they're smooth all right. Except they have a hard time with the fact that I'm asleep by 9:00 p.m. and up at five to ride Einstein. I've never had time for those games."

They did a quick whirl around the dance floor before the song concluded, and she reluctantly released his hand. "That was fun," she said.

"Don't sound so surprised."

"I'm pleasantly surprised. Is that better?" She didn't give him a chance to answer before she turned. "I'm going to grab another tea. Want one?"

"I can get us some," he said.

"Jess, I am capable of getting tea. Do you want a glass of tea or not?"

"Yeah, sure. Thanks." Jess stepped outside the warmth of the tent and took a deep breath as he stood in the cool June moonlight. The scent of roasting hot dogs teased him.

If someone had told him two months ago that he'd be dancing with his first crush come summer, he'd never have believed it.

"Look at you, dancing with Miss Kate," Willard said with a knowing grin.

Jess turned to see the old cowboy approach. "A two-step isn't really dancing. It's only slightly better than shuffling your feet." He glanced at Willard's attire. "You're dressed up tonight."

Willard straightened the silver bolo on his crisp white Western shirt and offered a wicked grin. "You gotta polish the feathers if you want to impress the chickens."

"Is that so?" Jess chuckled. "Any chickens in particular?"

"Pshaw. A gentleman never tells." Willard paused and blinked with surprise. "Well, I'll be."

"What?"

"Lookee there," Willard said. "Over by the firepit in those rockers set close together."

"What am I looking at?"

"Your sister and Finn."

"What?" Jess's gaze followed Willard's. Sure enough, Nicole and Finn Hardy each sat in a rocker, talking and smiling. And here he'd thought Finn was talking about Kate.

"Ain't love grand?" Willard said the words with a smile.

To his knowledge, his sister hadn't looked at another man since her husband's defection. She'd been gun-shy for the last two years, steering clear of romantic entanglements. Jess shook his head. He didn't know if he should be thrilled or concerned.

"Looks to me like he's wooing your sister."

Jess jerked back at the comment. "He's what?"

Willard chuckled. "*Wooing.* You even know what that is? Most of you young 'uns think romance has to do with phones, computers and dating apps."

"Okay, I'll bite. Tell me, what exactly is *wooing*, Willard?"

The cowboy pushed back his black Stetson and gave a musing smile. "Wooing takes a whole lot more energy than dating. It's about gaining someone's trust and confidence. Wooing is all about the long haul. It's like preparing the soil and planting, and being willing to wait for what's going to grow because you know it's going to be something special."

"Wooing." Jess rolled the word on his tongue. Would wooing have any effect on Kate? Was she even interested in the long haul? She'd been here since early spring, and it was now closing in on summer, yet she'd given no indication that she'd be around come autumn.

"Miss Kate is worth that. Don'tcha think?"

Jess stared at Willard. Was the cowboy reading his mind?

"You know, you're an interesting guy, Cornell. Most of the time, what comes out of your mouth rides a stream of malarkey. Though every now and then, you sound almost wise."

"That's some kind of backhanded compliment." Willard gave a hearty laugh. "You put your boot in your mouth like that with women too? It's no wonder you spend your free time with cattle."

"Hi, Willard. Having fun?" Both Willard and Jess turned at Kate's voice.

"I am now. By the way, Miss Kate, you're looking lovely tonight. I suppose all the cowboys already mentioned that." He stared pointedly at Jess before tipping his hat. "I best grab some food before it disappears. 'Scuse me, you two."

"What was that all about?" Kate handed him a tea.

"I'm never really sure with Willard, but he's right about one thing."

"What's that?"

"I haven't mentioned how nice you look tonight. I apologize for the omission."

She glanced down at herself. "Seriously? It's a skirt and a denim jacket."

"That's right, and you're the prettiest girl in a denim jacket at the Rebel Ranch hoedown. Accept the compliment."

"I, um, thank you." She paused. "Did you notice Finn and your sister?"

"I did, and then I glanced away."

"Why?" She smiled. "It's so sweet. They're a good match."

"What makes you say that?"

Kate shrugged. "I don't know. You can just tell. There's a specialness between them."

"A specialness?"

"I can't define it. It's a connection. The way they look at each other and communicate without words. You can just tell."

"Humph, all I can tell is that if he hurts my sister, he might inspire me to show him my own brand of specialness."

"Oh, cut it out. Now you sound like my brothers. There isn't a man alive that they approve of."

"No one?"

"Well, maybe one. Willard Cornell would pass muster."

Jess chuckled. "I fully side with your brothers."

Kate's eyes rounded and she perked up as the band struck up another number. "Listen. Do you hear that? I haven't heard that song in years. Probably since high school."

"Face it. We're getting old, Kate."

"You are," she said. "I'm still a kid."

"I'm only a few months older than you."

"And yet you already have those tiny little lines around your eyes." She touched his face, and he took her hand. Time froze as he continued to hold her hand, liking the feel of her soft skin against his.

"Those are laugh lines," he finally said. "I'm a happy guy." Yeah, he was a happy guy. Happier than he'd been in a very long time.

Kate released a small gasp. "Oh my, Jess. Will you look at who just showed up?"

Jess turned. "There's about half the town here tonight. You're going to have to be more specific."

"Franny Cox. Over by the registration table. Talking to Reece." As she said the words, Reece pointed in their direction. Franny waved enthusiastically and started to weave through the guests toward them.

"Franny!" Kate grabbed the older woman in a hug. "What are you doing here? Where's Rex?"

"At the last minute, my dear husband decided to stay home." Franny reached out to shake Jess's hand. "Good to see you, Jess."

"You too, Ms. Cox."

"Franny." She grinned, tipped back her cowboy hat, and looked Kate up and down. "Rebel Ranch agrees with you. I've never seen you looking so good. Why, you're positively glowing, young lady."

"Thank you, Franny. I feel good too," Kate said. "What's going on? I thought you weren't taking off for another week or two?"

"I got antsy. Decided to hit a little rodeo outside OK City. Thought I'd hang around until Sunday or Monday and maybe talk you into coming with me. You know, the assistant position I mentioned."

Kate shot Jess a quick glance, and in that moment, he saw the guilt on her face. He realized he'd been right all along. She was going to leave.

"I can't make any promises, Franny," Kate said. "I told you that. I haven't had time to think that far down the road yet."

"I get that. I'll give my sales pitch, and

you do what you've gotta do. Then I'll be on my way. Fair enough?"

Jess observed the exchange in silence as a dark cloud of foreboding settled over the evening.

"I'll let you two catch up," he said to Kate. "Miss Franny, I'm sure I'll see you again before you leave. In the meantime, be sure Kate takes you to the mess hall for a taste of Chef Luna's kickoff menu."

"Thanks, Jess," Franny said. "I'll do that."

Kate put a hand on his sleeve, and he paused. The blue eyes reflected concern. "Jess, I, um, thanks."

"Thanks? I didn't do anything, did I?" He offered a short nod before he stepped away. As he walked, he checked his phone. It was after eight, which meant he was officially off duty and no longer obligated to the ranch.

"Better grab yourself some food before it disappears," Willard said as he passed him.

"Yeah. I'll do that." Jess detoured at the stables, ducked behind the barn and went on to the parking area. It was time to call it a night.

Franny Cox's appearance meant only one thing. Kate was leaving. What did he expect? Kate was never going to stay in Rebel long enough to put down roots. Did he think their renewed friendship would even matter in the scheme of things? He wasn't a young, naive kid any longer. Falling for Kate again would be asking for heartache. Good thing he had no plans to let down his guard. No, this time, he was in control of his emotions. He wouldn't be blindsided twice in a lifetime.

Chapter Ten

Franny's trailer passed the feed-store delivery truck on the way down Rebel Ranch drive toward the main road. One going and one coming. Kate waved as the trailer rumbled away, the hitch clanging at the bumps on the road. She hated to see her friend leave. Franny had been like a big sister to her for so very long. A mentor on the circuit, as well. Now she was more lost and confused than ever.

Was she ready to close the door on this chapter of her life? That was a looming question. This time back in Oklahoma was supposed to be a detour, not her future. But with the neurologist's words, everything had changed. It hadn't become real until Franny's trailer lumbered away down the ranch road.

She would never compete again. Never ride a barrel again. Should she settle for being part of the circuit in an ancillary capacity as Franny's assistant or make a clean break and start over at Rebel Ranch?

Walking away from the circuit also meant the end of her search for her father. Looking for him on the internet had never proved successful. Her only hope was to walk in his boots. She'd been doing that for ten years. Was this the end of the line?

There were more questions than answers of late.

Kate stepped aside when the feed-store truck beeped while backing into position along the paved walkway.

"Want some help with that?"

She turned around, surprised to see Jess. "Oh, no, but thanks. We have a system. He loads the bags onto the hand truck I have parked over there, and I roll it into the storage shed."

Jess cocked his head. "How do the bags get from the hand truck to the shelf?"

Kate raised a hand and wiggled her fingers. "I put them there."

"It'll go faster with help."

"I have this. I'll save asking for help for when I really need it."

"Will you?"

"Yes. I will." Kate pushed back her hat and looked up to find him staring intently.

He glanced down the ranch drive. "Franny headed out?"

"Mmm-hmm. On her way to Oklahoma City."

"You're not going with her?"

"Not at the moment. I have things to do here," Kate said.

"I see." He gave a thoughtful nod. "Did she have a good time while she was here?"

"Yes. It was fun showing Franny around the ranch and downtown Rebel. We looked for you at the mess hall on Saturday and Sunday."

"I got tied up. A couple of issues to deal with."

She nodded. He'd disappeared as soon as Franny arrived on Friday night. He was nowhere to be found all weekend, despite his insistence she should be around for Chef Luna Diaz's special menu. He hadn't even been around on Saturday when she gave Olive her first horse-riding lesson.

"You missed the staff meeting this morning," Jess said.

Kate tensed. "I had an early appointment at the clinic."

"Are you sick?"

"No, I'm absolutely healthy." She swallowed, gathering courage. "Jess, do you think we could talk?"

"Talk? What about?"

"Stop by the house after work, and I'll tell you."

He frowned. "Aren't we talking right now?"

"It seems like we're always discussing important things on the run. I'd like to sit down and have a discussion."

"Important things?" He raised his brows in question.

Kate nearly stomped her foot at his obtuseness. "Stop repeating what I say. Will you or will you not stop by after work?"

Jess chuckled. "Okay, I'll be there."

"Great."

"Great in theory," Kate muttered hours later. Today was absolutely the time to talk to him about his mother. So why was her stomach in turmoil? Because she had no idea what his response would be. She kept a close eye on the clock in her closet office as she rehearsed over and over in her head what she would say to Jess.

Jess, I'm donating a kidney to your mother. Jess, how much do you know about living-donor transplantation?

Once she talked to him, she planned to speak to each of her brothers on the phone, giving them her prepared speech. Yes, doing it on the phone was cowardly, but she'd learned long ago that it was the least confrontational route with them.

Kate's phone vibrated on her desk, stirring her from deep thoughts. She checked the screen. A text from Franny. She'd arrived in Oklahoma City and had run into several mutual friends who sent their regards. Nostalgia washed over Kate at the words and stayed with her most of the afternoon.

At five o'clock, Kate closed her laptop and waved goodbye to Violet as she left the admin building. The short walk to her house provided an opportunity to clear her mind and say a short prayer.

Jess was prompt and showed up at five fifteen.

"Come on in," she called at the knock on the door.

Jess stepped inside. Still in his work clothes, she couldn't help but admire how nicely the black Rebel Ranch T-shirt looked on the man. He held a bag from Daisy's bakery in one hand as he looked around.

"Whoa. Your house smells like supper hour at the diner. What are you cooking?"

The scents wafting through the house were enticing, and Kate could barely believe she was responsible for them.

"Cheesy chicken and broccoli. It's a recipe from the cookbook you gave me." She couldn't help a shy smile. "I can't tell you how much my life has changed since you and Olive introduced me to the slow cooker. I always thought things like that would be challenging for me. All these years, I could have used it in the motor home."

"Thinking about going out on the road again, are you?"

"That was a general observation." She hoped to avoid a discussion of her long-term plans. "You stopped by the bakery?"

"No. I ran into Daisy on my way here. Sometimes she brings extra baked goods to the ranch." He held up the bag. "I scored muffins for you."

"Thank you." She turned and nodded down the hall. "Let's go into the kitchen."

"I'm not sure that's safe. I may want to steal your dinner."

"That's the idea. Maybe we could call this a pop quiz. You taste test and let Olive know if I pass."

"I like the sound of that," he said with a grin.

"Me too. Have a seat."

He shook his head. "I'll set the table. I should at least work for my supper."

Kate pointed left. "Over there. Above the stove. We'll need bowls."

Jess opened the cupboard. "Hey, these look familiar. You got these from Nicole's shop."

"Yes. Aren't they pretty? They match the mugs." She gestured toward the patio door. "Mind if we sit outside?"

"Sure, but first you have to tell me what this is." He picked up the glossy ceramic hand on the table and turned it over, examining the piece from all sides.

"You don't recognize that?"

"It's a hand. I know that much."

"It's Olive's hand. She made it in your sister's shop and gave it to me."

"Ahh, now that you mention it, this does look familiar." He chuckled. "What did you do to deserve such a prize?"

"It's a thank-you for her first riding lesson."

His head jerked up, and he pinned her

with a surprised gaze. "How did I miss that?"

"You tell me. You were on the schedule for Saturday, but I guess you traded with someone."

Jess frowned. "I, um, I needed a break."

A break from her? Kate stared at him for a moment. What had she done to alienate him? Things had been going so well at the hoedown. Until Franny arrived. Had things changed because Franny had offered her a job?

"You sure are thinking hard," he said.

"I'm wondering if maybe Olive and I will see you around this Saturday for her second lesson."

"Sure. I'd like to see my niece in the saddle. How'd she do?"

Kate held a trivet close to her and smiled. "Oh, Jess. You'd be so proud. She's a natural. I can see her barrel racing someday."

"Yeah?" His angular face lit up, and a spark ignited in the gray eyes. "Tell me about it."

"I don't know where to begin." She

paused. "Olive is fearless. She loves horses, and they love her. There's a confidence about her in the saddle that amazes me."

"I'll stop by on Saturday," he said. "And, Kate, thanks for doing this."

"It really was a pleasure. Seeing someone so enthusiastic and with such passion reminded me of when I was a kid." She opened a drawer and removed silverware.

"I've got that."

Careful not to touch Jess, she handed him the silverware and cloth napkins.

"Can I get you some tea?" she asked.

"Sure."

Kate's hands shook as she poured the store-bought tea into two glasses and brought them outside. At times like this, she realized how socially backward she really was. Thirty years old, and she'd never had a man over for dinner.

Once Jess brought the slow-cooker pot to the table, Kate reached for the bowls.

"Oh, man. You better ladle faster. The smell of that is killing me. I'm starving," he said. "I had a fast sandwich hours ago for lunch."

Kate laughed, pleased at his eagerness. "Here you go."

"Thank you." He reached for her hand, bowed his head and said a quick prayer before Kate knew what was happening.

"Amen," she murmured, her pulse still racing from his hand holding hers.

"Look at that sky," Jess said. He folded a napkin on his lap while his gaze inspected the expanse of darkening horizon visible from the covered patio.

"Those are rain clouds to the north. It's coming in fast." She inhaled. "Smells loamy, doesn't it?"

"Yep. Boy, could we use the moisture," Jess observed.

"What's the contingency plan for entertaining guests when it rains at Rebel Ranch?" Kate asked.

"Mitch has backup activities in the admin building. I heard it rained a week straight last year, and he brought in a few local artisans for classes. My sister taught pottery classes."

"That's genius."

"Yeah, it really went over well with the guests."

A comfortable silence enveloped them as they ate, and while Kate was grateful not to have to attempt small talk, she kept sneaking peeks at Jess. The man kept eating, even going for second helpings of the meal. Was he being kind, or was it really palatable? Sure, she liked it, but her bar was pretty low.

"Does that second helping mean I passed the test?" she asked.

Jess leaned back and patted his stomach. "Seriously, Kate? This is amazing. I'm totally satiated. And now that you've plied me with chicken, you better tell me what you wanted to discuss before I take a nap right here."

A crack of thunder interrupted their conversation, followed by a kick of wind that set the hammock in motion.

"Looks like it's coming sooner than later," Jess said.

When rain began to spit down, Kate stood. "Are your windows rolled up?" she asked.

"No. I'll be right back."

Fat drops began to hit the cement pathway to the patio, and Kate grabbed the slow cooker and headed inside, as well. When Jess returned a moment later, his face and shirt were wet. He placed his damp hat on the doorknob.

Kate pulled a towel from the drawer. There was another crack of thunder, and she jumped, dropping the terry cloth. When they both reached for it at the same time, Jess placed his hands on her shoulders. Mesmerized by the drops of moisture on his long lashes, she stared at the prism of colors in his irises as he steadied her.

She swallowed, unable to keep her gaze from moving to his mouth as her pulse galloped away.

"I got this," Jess said, his voice shaky. "We don't need another head knock."

"Right," she murmured.

He picked up the towel and wiped the rain from his face.

"The wind has slowed," Kate said. "Let's go back on the patio." She certainly could use a bit of air right now.

Jess sat down on the glider, and Kate eased onto the other end, as far away as she could. Once set in motion, the glider creaked gently as it moved back and forth.

"Needs lubricating oil. I'll bring some by next time," he said.

Next time. Would there be a next time? Would she even be around for a next time?

Her glance followed his as he looked toward the yard where a steady curtain of rain continued, cocooning them on all sides.

"So what was it you wanted to talk about?" Jess asked.

Kate bit her lip, not eager to end the companionable mood between them. "A couple of medical things have come up," she finally said while searching for the words. Her planned speech seemed to have disappeared.

He turned, immediately focused on her words. "Are you having dizzy spells again?"

"I'm fine, Jess. Actually, I'm so fine that

I discussed testing to be a kidney donor with my doctor. It turns out that I qualify as a match for your mother."

Jess opened his mouth, and his jaw slacked. He stared at her for a long minute.

"Say something," she murmured. His silence hung in the air ominously.

"I don't know what to say." Jess ran a hand over his face. "How long have you known this?"

"Since before the hoedown."

"And you didn't see fit to discuss this with me? I thought you and I..." He released a pained breath.

Kate listened to him stumble around defining what exactly they were. Friends? Surely more than that? But what?

"To be clear," she finally said. "This isn't about you and me. This was my decision to make." She clasped her hands in her lap. "And I'm discussing it with you now."

"Kate, you've been in and out of clinics and hospitals since February. Why would you purposely put yourself in that position again?"

"How can I not? And what better time than now when my life is at a crossroads? There's nowhere I have to be. I don't have a clue what's next for me. Everything lined up for this moment, as though this is the perfect time."

When he didn't answer, she leaned forward, trying to understand what he was thinking as she assessed the somber gray eyes. "Are you mad?" she asked.

"Mad, no. Confused would be closer. Real confused." He looked at her. "Mind if I ask you where you'll be come fall?"

"I can't tell you what's in the future. The last decade has been spent tracking my father on the circuit. It's the only life I've ever known."

He released a deep breath. "I take it you and my mother have already discussed this?"

"Yes. I've talked to her. I also talked to my doctor this morning. I passed the psych evaluation, and they're ready to schedule surgery. There's no turning back in my mind. My decision is made."

"I've done a decent amount of research

into this myself, Kate. What if you get cold feet? Or worse, what if you regret the choice afterward? Lots of people have donor remorse."

"Not me. Once you've looked death in the eye, your entire attitude shifts."

He continued to stare at her. "Your mother passed from cancer. What if you need that other kidney?"

"You aren't making any sense." She shook her head. "My mother's cancer had nothing to do with her kidneys. It was a rare type of gene mutation that isn't hereditary."

"What do your brothers say about this?"

"I plan to call each of them separately."

"Not in person?"

"Do you know how difficult it is to get them alone? Besides their individual families, the Farmers Market has started, Ballard B&B opened, not to mention the ranch schedule is in full swing. Tucker has two adoption events scheduled."

"You know they're going to push back." He shook his head.

"I don't usually make decisions by committee, Jess. And make no mistake, this is my decision. I hope that you and my brothers will support me."

"And if I don't?"

She paused at his words and lowered her head. "I'll be disappointed, but I'm still moving forward. I've spent a good deal of time in prayer and research, and I believe it's what my mother would want me to do. Perhaps in some way, this is how I'm honoring her. I have perfect peace."

Perfect peace, yet deep down inside, she still sought Jess's approval. Probably more so than her brothers'. She cared what he thought far more than she should, maybe because she cared about him far more than she should.

"What's got you in knots, McNally?" Willard asked. The old cowboy took a T-post driver to a pole and glanced over at Jess.

"I'm not in knots."

"Sure you are. You've been staring at that

fence wire for a good five minutes. You can't tighten fencing by watching it."

Willard had accompanied him to do a fence check in preparation for a cattle drive that included Rebel Ranch guests. They'd move the cattle from the back of the ranch to the seeded grazing paddock with native forage closer to the barns.

Jess wiped the sweat from his face and adjusted his gloves. Willard was right. He'd been caught up thinking, and he wasn't paid to think about Kate during work hours. Yet his gut had been churning for the last twenty-four hours, since he'd found out about her plans. He'd seen Kate battered, bruised and in pain, and he sure didn't want to see her put her life on the line again.

He twisted the fence wire into a Z with his pliers, starting at the top and going to the bottom. Then he stood and looked over at Willard. "What time is it?"

"Nearly dinner, and Chef Luna has pulled-pork carnitas on the menu tonight. I think I smell them already."

"Sorry to miss that, but I've got an appointment after work."

"More for me." Willard rested his arms on the post and looked over at Jess. "How's that wooing coming along?"

"You practice being random or does it just come naturally?" Jess asked.

"I guess it's not going so well," Willard muttered. He picked up the T-post driver and shoved it in the back of the UTV. "We're done here. I guess I'll see you tomorrow. Maybe whatever's eating at you will have passed by then."

"See you tomorrow," Jess mumbled.

Dust billowed along the trail as Willard took off in the vehicle, and for a minute, Jess simply stared out across the land. He'd been orderly and deliberate in the last few months, since returning to Rebel. How had everything gotten out of control?

Jess mounted his horse and headed to the stable.

After a quick washup, he grabbed his hat and wasted no time heading into town to his mother's house. She opened the door on the first knock, her face brightening. "Jess, did I know you were coming?"

"No. Is this a bad time?"

She adjusted the ends of the scarf around her neck and checked her appearance in the hall mirror. "I'm out the door shortly for choir practice, but I always have time for my favorite son."

He couldn't help but smile as he followed her into the living room. "This won't take long. I tried to reach you last night, but you didn't answer. Nicole said you were at mahjong."

"Oh, yes, sorry. It lasted much too late. I started chatting with Magnolia Parker about her new grandbaby and lost all track of time." She turned. "Why didn't you leave a message? I would have called you back."

"I wanted to talk to you in person."

"Uh-oh, this sounds serious. Let's sit down." She perched on the couch and looked at him expectantly.

He couldn't sit. The pent-up energy inside him was ready to explode. Instead, he paced back and forth on the braided rug before facing his mother. "Kate is donating a kidney." Simply uttering those words was painful and caused a domino of unspeakable aches inside his chest. "Why didn't you tell me?"

"She asked me not to. Kate wanted to be the one to tell you."

"Mom, I moved back home to take care of you. I think I should have been let in on the discussion."

"Jess, you're a wonderful son, and I appreciate everything you do for me. However, it's not your job to take care of me. Nor was it your job to take care of your father."

"Maybe if I'd been here instead of in Montana, I could have done something. Maybe we wouldn't have lost Dad." Jess clenched his hands at his sides as he spoke, all the while struggling to keep the emotions bubbling inside him at bay.

His mother's eyes rounded. "Oh, my, is that what's been keeping you up at night?"

"I left Oklahoma because he and I didn't agree on my future. I shouldn't have let that keep me away. If only…" He shook his head, unable to finish the thought as anguish choked him.

"Your father was a proud and stubborn man. I'm sorry he never admitted that he was wrong. But he was, and he knew it. Both you and Nicole had the right to your own futures, not the ones he'd planned for you. Just remember that he believed you both could do anything, and he wanted the best for you."

"Yeah, I realize that now. Much too late. I should have come home more often. Been here for you both." A searing pain shot through him at the admission.

"Is that what this is all about? You believe that you let your father down? Is that why you want to keep tight control on my life?"

"I love you, Mom."

"Yes, and I love you too. But we're human. These mortal bodies will fail, and it certainly won't be your fault." She sighed. "While I admit I long to be around to see you marry and see your first child, I'm also at all times ready for a greater calling. One that doesn't include this life on earth."

"Don't talk like that. You're way too young to leave us."

"Perhaps, but as we know, life isn't always fair." She paused. "Now, maybe you can explain to me why you don't think Kate donating a kidney is a good idea."

He couldn't answer. Couldn't tell her what he felt, because he wasn't sure.

"I can make an educated guess," she said. "Perhaps you think it's not a good idea because Kate is the woman you're in love with."

Jess's head snapped up at the words. "No. I'm not in love with Kate. I've been very careful not to cross that line."

His mother nodded slowly, as though considering his words. "I can see you have your mind convinced, but I'm not sure your heart understands the rules, dear."

Had he been lying to himself? Was he denying how he felt so he wouldn't get hurt again?

"Jess?"

He didn't know what to say. Kate was sacrificing to save his mother. What if something happened to her? To his mother? Surgery had no guarantees.

He loved them both too much to consider losing either of them.

Jess swallowed. *He loved Kate.* The thought hit him like a rolling bale of hay. He ran a hand over his face.

"So, this really is news to you?" his mother asked. "That you're still in love with her?"

Pain, like a punch in the gut, hit him at her words. "Kate's not sticking around."

"Maybe if you ask her to, she will."

"How I feel isn't going to change her plans."

"You don't know that. You're both older, and, I hope, a lot smarter." She paused. "Does she know how you feel?"

No. Kate didn't know how he felt, because up to this very moment, he hadn't had the courage to admit to himself that for the second time in his life, he was in love with the woman who held the power to break his heart.

Chapter Eleven

K ate opened the front door to find all of her brothers on the stoop. She offered a sigh of exasperation and leaned on the door jamb while looking at the handsome faces of Mitch, Reece and Tucker.

Though she'd called and spoken to each one individually, they'd still decided to respond with a group effort. She'd expected kickback. They were her brothers, after all. But did it have to be so early in the morning?

"I can't begin to tell you how good it makes me feel to have you all on my doorstep at 7:00 a.m. on a Saturday." A yawn escaped.

"Were you sleeping?" Reece asked.

"No, but it's my day off." Her gaze assessed the trio again. "It's your day off too, and you have families who want your attention."

"Bug, we're here because we have a few items to discuss with you," Mitch said. He wore his eldest-brother, serious-business face today.

Kate groaned. "You guys are going to have to stop this. You have your own families to deal with."

"Let me point out the obvious," Tucker said. "You are our family."

"Fine." Kate unlocked the screen and walked to the kitchen. Why fight the inevitable? She would always be the little sister, and her turning thirty hadn't changed their overprotective natures.

"Where's Bella?" Tucker asked, glancing around.

"Probably on the window ledge in my bedroom planning world domination." She grabbed a can of Dr. Pepper from the fridge as she stepped into the kitchen. "Help yourselves."

Reece reached in, took three bottled waters and passed them out to his brothers.

When Kate put a package of store-bought sandwich cookies on the table, Mitch looked from the package to her. "It's 7:00 a.m."

"If you were expecting breakfast, you're at the wrong house. I've come a long way, but eggs and I are still not on speaking terms."

"You drink soda for breakfast?" Reece asked.

Kate glared at him. "Are you guys really here to evaluate my dietary habits?" She pointed to her shiny, new, stainless steel slow cooker on the counter. "Because I'm actually a changed woman. I have appliances, and I know how to use them."

Tucker's brows lifted. "It does smell awfully good in here, now that you mention it."

"Chili in the slow cooker. Tonight's dinner."

"I'm impressed," he said.

"Wonderful. Now tell me why you're here," Kate said. "I don't mean to rush you or anything, but I have important plans with Olive at nine."

"Who's Olive?" Reece asked.

"Jess's niece. We have a riding lesson."

"That's great, Kate. You know, we've been hearing great things about the equine program from our guests. Those gals you hired are top-notch," Reece said.

"Thank you." She held the praise from Reece close. It meant a lot. Perhaps she was making a difference at Rebel Ranch.

"So..." Mitch said. Hands steepled, he glanced at his brothers. "We're here to talk about the kidney-donating thing."

"Yeah," Reece burst out. "You gave us a heads-up on the phone, Kate." He ran a hand over the dark shadow of beard on his face. "That was kinda below the belt, don't you think?"

Kate dropped into a chair and frowned, because they were right. She had taken the cowardly route. "I'm sorry," she murmured. "That was the chicken way out. But I won't be changing my mind about the surgery. I am absolutely certain this is what I'm supposed to do."

"Susan McNally is a good person," Mitch

agreed. "The Rainbolts are beholden to her for the many times she stepped in quietly behind the scenes after Mom passed. That doesn't mean you owe her a kidney."

"This isn't about paying a debt," Kate said. "This is about how sometimes you just know you're on the correct path."

When Reece opened his mouth in protest, she held up a hand. "I've done the research. I've even had a session with a former donor and a counselor. I'm going into this with knowledge." She took a breath as she searched for the words. "In the end, it was in the quiet moments that I knew this decision was absolutely right."

The only sound in the little kitchen was the measured ticks of the wall clock. Kate didn't dare look at her brothers. Would they continue to push back against what she knew she should do?

"Kate, you're all we have," Reece finally murmured.

"And you are all I have. But after thirty years, surely you've realized that I'll never be the Rainbolt who plays it safe." She took a deep breath as the shadow of grief blanketed her. "Playing it safe provides no guarantees anyhow. We know that."

"Isn't that the truth?" Tucker reached across the table for the cookies and shoved two in his mouth.

Kate immediately regretted her words. Her brothers were silent at the subtle reference to the loss of the youngest Rainbolt sibling, Levi, in an auto accident and the untimely death of Tucker's first wife.

"I'm sorry, Tucker," she said softly.

He shrugged. "Apology not necessary. You're right, Kate. There are no guarantees, but that doesn't mean we are going to worry any less about you."

"Does this mean the three of you are going to support my decision?"

Tucker pointedly met the eyes of his big brothers. "I believe we're moving to that place."

"I checked the schedule and noticed you're taking a week off," Mitch said. "Does that have something to do with the surgery?"

"No, the tentative date for the surgery is September. I'm going to spend a few days with my friend, Franny. You remember her. The barrel racer who was here for the hoedown."

Mitch took a long swig of water before he spoke. "Are you thinking about going back on the road? Back to the rodeo?"

"No way," Tucker said. "Not a career path for a woman with one kidney."

Kate pulled back her frustration. Here they were, treating her like a kid again instead of a woman who understood the impact of her decisions. "If I returned to the rodeo, it would not be in the arena."

"That's good to hear," Mitch said.

"No plans have been made, dear brother. I'm going to hang out with Franny to simply take a break and evaluate things."

"While you're evaluating, please remember that we want you to stay in Rebel," Reece said.

"I appreciate that," Kate said a little more gently. "I'm exploring all my options."

"Is this about TJ?" Mitch asked. "This exploring-your-options stuff?"

"That's part of it. I'm reevaluating my life. Don't tell me you all haven't come to a crossroads a time or two in your lives?"

Tucker, Reece and Mitch each gave a slow nod of agreement.

"That's where I am," she said. "I've spent my life on a quest to find answers, and I'm beginning to realize that I've wasted too much time. My father, my flesh and blood, didn't care enough to stay. All this time, I wanted to believe there was a deeper reason." She shrugged. "There wasn't."

"I like to be kinder to the old man," Mitch said. "He didn't have the ability to care enough."

"That's quite the spin," Kate said, unable to prevent the bitter tone that underlined her words.

"It's the one I can live with. I try to remember that his departure taught us all a valuable life lesson. Compassion. Toward each other and others. Rainbolts know what it's like to be on the outside looking in, and that's why we will never treat others like we were treated."

"I can agree with that," Kate said. "Which is why I'm donating my kidney to Susan McNally. Compassion toward others. As you said, it's something others didn't always have for us, because we were the kids left behind."

Just saying the words was enough to tighten her chest as she recalled the hard times they'd gone through together. Kate looked at each of her brothers and found herself remorseful. "I'm so sorry. I didn't mean to bring up the past."

"This conversation is long overdue," Reece said. "We've all been pretending that if we don't talk about the past, it didn't happen. But it did. Clearing the air is a good thing."

"Reece is right. We need to talk. Then we need to move on," Mitch said. He paused and looked around the table at everyone. "Confession time."

All eyes turned to Mitch.

"After the twins were born, I hired a private detective to check on Dad." He ran a hand over his face. "All those years in law enforcement, I could have looked into it, but I was afraid to. Afraid of what I might find. Suddenly, when I had my own children, their heritage and the legacy that would be passed down to them became important. The fact that we have no family except each other hit me hard for the first time since Mom died."

"What did you find out?" Kate asked. She gripped the edge of the table, waiting for his answer.

"Not a thing. It's been twenty-two years since he took off. That trail is cold."

"Nothing?" Kate murmured. "No records anywhere?"

"Nope. I can verify that." Reece cleared his throat. "I'll admit, I checked too. Paid for those online database searches, and I asked a friend in the Oklahoma Bureau of Investigation to take a peek. Nothing. He wasn't a veteran, and he didn't have a criminal record, so he managed to fly under the radar."

"The man doesn't want to be found," Tucker said.

"Or maybe he died," Mitch said solemnly.

"I don't want him to have passed," Kate said. She bit back tears as her thoughts swirled. What she wanted was the chance to find out why he left. To find out why he couldn't be her father.

Reece inched closer and put a big hand over hers. "More than likely, he's sitting on a beach in Mexico."

"The fact is, each of us was touched by Mama's death and Daddy's defection, but it doesn't have to rule our life," Mitch said. "One thing I learned in sessions with that therapist is that life isn't like movies. It's not fair, and there is no guarantee of happily-ever-after on this Earth. What is promised is our eternal happiness."

"Easy to say," Kate said.

"Maybe. Or maybe you should consider the fact that you had something that no other little girl had."

Kate cocked her head in question. "What's that?"

"Three fathers," Mitch continued. "Three voices in your head warning you that if you missed curfew, even thought about picking up tobacco, sneaking into a club with a fake ID, or any other rite of passage, your three dads would know. Know and lower the boom faster than you could say 'You're ruining my life.'"

Laughter bubbled up, and Kate released it and let go of the tension that had held her rigid. "You do have a point." She sucked in a ragged breath. "Which is probably why my most memorable act of rebellion was toilet papering Pastor Young's house."

"You forced the man into early retirement, as I recall. After he denounced the act of a hooligan from the pulpit." Mitch grinned.

"Oh, that's not true. He was well overdue for retirement."

Both Tucker and Reece chuckled.

"We should have had this talk long ago," Mitch said. "I'll be the first to admit that there was no way I was emotionally ready to deal with the past until I started seeing a counselor." He paused. "I think we should focus on the fact that we're building something new here in Rebel. A new heritage for our families. For ourselves."

"I agree." Reece looked at his watch. "Though I'm running out of time at the moment. I promised Claire I'd give her some time off and watch the kids."

"A final thought before we leave," Mitch said. "I've been praying about something for a while. When I chatted with Kate a few weeks ago, she mentioned that Mom was accepted into nursing school and couldn't attend because she was pregnant with me."

"Mom wanted to go into the medical field?" Tucker perked up.

Mitch nodded. "Yeah. Since she's the real hero of our story, I thought we could honor her. What about a nursing scholarship in her name at OSU?" He looked at Tucker. "You're teaching there. I'm guessing you could help us with that."

"I'm one hundred percent on board," Tucker said with a grin.

"Mitch, that's a wonderful idea," Kate added. "I've had another thought, as well. Actually, it was Jess's idea."

"Oh?" Mitch nodded for her to proceed.

"Have you thought about a youth rodeo in the summer? Maybe to honor Levi?"

"I like it. I like it a lot," Mitch said. "Of course, you'd have to stick around to make that happen, and you'd have to be willing to manage the rodeo but not participate."

"I'll keep that in mind as I pray about the future," Kate said.

"Speaking of prayer," Reece said. "We need to start praying collectively for you and Susan McNally." He stood and pushed in his chair.

"Good plan," Mitch said.

Tucker looked pointedly at Kate. "We'll want plenty of heads-up so we can be at the hospital."

"Absolutely," Kate said.

"Seems fitting that we end this therapy session with a group prayer," Mitch said with a wink.

Kate nodded. "Yes," she said softly.

Standing, each took the hand of the sibling next to them and then bowed their heads.

"Tucker, you pray," Mitch said.

"Lord, I thank You for the blessings You've given the Rainbolt family these many years. You have guided us each day, and I ask You to continue to do that. Bless Rebel Ranch and show us how we can serve Your Kingdom. Protect and keep Kate and Susan McNally as they prepare for surgery. Direct Kate's step where You lead her. Take care of our sister, Lord. We love her so much. Amen."

Kate hugged each of her brothers, grateful for the unconditional love they gave so freely. She'd taken them for granted for far too long. Now all she had to do was figure out if she had the courage to give up the life she'd built for herself over the last ten years and start over at Rebel Ranch. She didn't know the answer to that question yet.

"Uncle Jess! Over here!"

Jess grinned at the sight of Olive standing in the circular pen next to a pretty paint, with Kate at her side.

"Nice helmet you've got there, kiddo," he called.

"Thanks, Uncle Jess. Miss Kate bought it for me." She lifted her feet one at a time, kicking at the red Oklahoma dirt. "Look at this, Momma bought me new boots too."

"You're a real rider now," he said. "How are you feeling? A little nervous?"

"I was last week," Olive admitted. She fingered the strap of her helmet and gave a little shrug of her thin shoulders. "But now I'm friends with Rosie. That's my horse. I'm so excited."

Jess couldn't help but smile again. Olive had spoken more words in the last few minutes than she usually did in an entire afternoon.

"Good for you," he said. He turned to Kate. "Has she learned to groom and tack up, yet?"

"Yes, sir," Kate said. "She and I did that together last Saturday and today."

Olive beamed. "It was fun."

Kate stood with a hand on the reins as she looked at Olive proudly. "Let's review what we discussed last week."

"Move real quiet and real slow."

"Right," Kate said. "Now we can prepare to ride."

Jess pulled the brim of his hat down against the June sun as he watched Kate guide Olive to double-check the cinch and stirrups. Then she helped Olive into the saddle.

His pride swelled when his niece sat tall on the paint. Pulling out his phone, he took a few pictures for Nicole and his mother.

"Remember," Kate said, "the reins are like the steering wheel and brakes, and your legs are the gas pedal. We're going to work on your driver's license this week."

Olive giggled as she sat in the saddle. "My driver's license."

Jess loped his arms over the fence to watch Olive and Rosie moving around the pen with Kate gently offering instruction. There was a slight breeze, and Kate's dark ponytail, tipped in purple, swayed as she walked alongside Olive.

It was hard to believe he was here on Rebel Ranch, with Kate teaching his niece how to ride. There was no way his happiness wouldn't be reflected on his face. His heart swelled with joy at the sight, and he didn't care who saw. Moments like this were something to tuck away for a lonely day.

"Is that your family?"

He turned at the voice, befuddled by the question. A middle-aged woman stood next to him at the fence, smiling. A ranch guest, no doubt.

"Ma'am?" Jess asked.

"I was saying that your wife and daughter are lovely," she continued. "How blessed you are."

The words tickled him, and he tipped his hat and nodded. "Blessed is what I am. Yes, ma'am."

Kate and Olive walked right past Jess and the woman as they circled the pen. Kate raised her brows, indicating that she had obviously overheard the conversation. Good. Maybe that might get her thinking about all the reasons why she should stay in Rebel.

"Is this where you sign up for lessons?" the woman continued. "I've heard some very good things about the guest riding program here."

"Yes, ma'am. Kate Rainbolt and her staff are responsible for the good things you've heard." He pointed to the guest stable. "There's someone right at the entrance who will get you all set up."

"Thank you, young man."

He turned back to the pen in time to see Kate wave her assistant over. "Olive, Joy is going to help you remove your tack and groom Rosie while I talk to your uncle Jess, okay?"

"Mmm-hmm."

Kate nodded to Joy, who led Olive out of the pen.

"Is she going to be okay with Joy? I mean, I thought Olive only wanted you," Jess said.

"She doesn't even know I'm here anymore. It's all about the horse."

"Oh, she knows you're here. You're the one who made this happen. She'll never forget. This is monumental. And Rosie is her first love. You never forget your first love." His gaze was focused on the horse as he said the words, though he couldn't deny it was the mango-scented woman next to him who'd inspired them.

She eyed him. "You're waxing poetic today. Have you been hanging around Willard?"

"I'm serious. Don't you remember your first horse?"

"As a matter of fact, I do. Mitch scraped together money so I could take lessons. That pony was named Pinto." She grinned, and her face lit up. "I loved that horse."

"There you go."

"So, Jess, why did you let that woman think that we're a family?" Kate looked at him.

"It made her happy, and she's a guest." He shrugged. "What can it hurt? Besides, we are family. We're all part of the Rebel Ranch family."

A bemused smile touched Kate's lips as he said the words.

"You know," he continued. "Olive is ten years old. Ever think that if you and I had ended up together, we might have had a kid about her age?"

Kate's blue eyes flew open, wide and panicked. "I—I…"

Her stunned expression gave him pause, but this time he wasn't sorry that what he'd been thinking had ended up on his lips. "Is that so shocking to consider?" he asked.

"No. That's not it. Or maybe it is. I don't know what to say to that, Jess."

"Nothing to say." Her response said it all. Apparently, he was the only one who took an occasional what-if stroll. And that was okay. Jess tucked his hands in his pockets. He was a patient man, and after ten years, what was one more day? He was starting to believe that Kate's return wasn't simply providence. Lately, as he considered the events of the last few months, he'd begun to believe that everything was working toward a purpose. So, yeah, he could wait it out and see what the good Lord had in mind.

"Now what are you thinking about?" she asked.

"Only good thoughts." He smiled. "When's your next session with Olive?"

"We've left it open. I'm heading out tomorrow to spend some time at a little rodeo north of Oklahoma City with Franny."

"Wait. You're leaving?" Her words whooshed the air from him, and he flinched as though he'd been punched in the gut. "When were you going to tell me?"

"I was going to let you know today. It's only for a week. I'd like to see if working as her assistant is something I want to do. I've also a few other offers to check out."

And just like that, all the maybes he'd started to hang his tomorrows on vanished. She was leaving again. "I thought you were done with rodeo?" he asked.

"I know that the arena isn't an option any longer. But rodeo has been my life for ten years. I've developed relationships, connections. I'm not sure I'm ready to walk away from that."

She paused. "You know, maybe it's time for you to reevaluate your own future, Jess. Your mother will be in a much better place health-wise after this surgery. You may be heading back to Montana."

"I'm not going anywhere, Kate. I'm staying in Rebel. I finally figured out that I want to be where my family is. Rebel is where I belong." Now all he had to do was convince her that it was where she belonged.

"That's great," she said with a gentle smile. "Perhaps you could extend me the same courtesy. I need a little space. I've been in a holding pattern since February, waiting for my body to heal, for my balance issues to subside. But I haven't stopped to take time to figure out what's next for me."

"A little space?" Like ten years hadn't been enough?

"Yes."

"Am I missing the signals here?" he asked softly. "Isn't there a little bit of you-and-me mixed into all this? Am I jumping the gun here, Kate? Is there even an *us*?"

She glanced away, as if hesitant to let him see what she was thinking. "I hope so, but I don't want to presume."

Jess placed his hand over hers where it

rested on the roughly hewn wood. "It's not presumptuous. I've tried to keep myself from caring for you, Kate. It's not working."

"Oh, Jess," she murmured. Pain touched the blue eyes as she looked at him. "That only tells me how much you don't trust me. You believe that I'd purposely hurt you."

She was right. For the last ten years, he'd had a standing policy of protecting himself from being gutted again, which had left him on the outside looking in when it came to relationships.

He met her gaze and forced himself to ask the question he wasn't sure he wanted the answer to. "So what's the future hold for us?"

She slipped her hand from beneath his and raised her palm in an I-don't-know gesture. "I keep saying the same thing, but you aren't listening. I don't know if Rebel Ranch is my future."

"Okay, forget me. What about my mom? What about the transplant?"

"I'll be back in time for the surgery."

Kate stared at him for a long moment. "Do you really think I'd let your mother down?"

"I didn't say that."

"Sure you did. That's exactly what you're thinking." She released a breath of frustration. "Every time I think you believe in me, you prove me wrong."

"You have to admit that you do have a track record of leaving."

"Leaving isn't the same as walking away. I left. My father walked away." She stiffened and crossed her arms. "For the record, I left once. I had a plan, and I followed my plan."

He nodded slowly, wanting desperately to understand. "Kate, if something happens while you're on the road or with Franny... The surgery..."

"It was my decision to donate, and I've jumped through quite a few hoops to do it, and I will follow through. I love your mom, and I'd never hurt her. You might want to consider getting your boots out of your mouth before you annoy me any further."

"I'm sorry. That came out wrong." How

could he tell her that his greatest fear was losing her or his mother? He was afraid and loathe to admit the fact.

As though defeated, Kate gave a weary sigh and slowly shook her head. "You're ready to think the worst of me, Jess. That's what hurts the most."

Jess could only stare at her, looking deep into her blue eyes as he worked to understand the puzzle of the woman before him.

It didn't take long to realize that the only thing he'd figured out was that he'd come full circle. His heart still galloped when she was near, and no matter how hard he resisted, he couldn't deny he was head over boots in love with the woman.

Yet here he stood, once again about to watch Kate Rainbolt walk away from him. Walk away with his heart.

Chapter Twelve

Another day, another rodeo. This was the second rodeo this week, and it only served to confirm the decision Kate had come to this morning. She sat in the bleachers letting the familiar buzz of the crowd, along with the smell of dirt, leather and animals soothe her as the crowd returned to their seats after intermission.

As usual, her gaze scanned the bleachers of the indoor facility as it began to fill up. Cowboys and cowgirls of all shapes and sizes entered, finding their seats once again and settling in for the action that would soon begin on the arena floor. Kate inspected each of them, as was her habit, hoping her gaze would land on a familiar face.

It was time to walk away from the search that had consumed her life for so long. She knew it in her heart, yet every single time she made a mental step forward to thoughts of a new life, fear yanked her back to the life she'd known.

"Kate!"

She turned and stood at Franny's familiar voice. Her friend wore a grin as wide as the cowboy hat perched on the back of her head. She bounded down the steps toward Kate. Her trademark rhinestone-studded Western shirt and oversize trophy buckle sparkled in the sunshine.

"Franny, why aren't you getting ready for your event?"

"I just wanted to check on you."

"Me? I'm fine."

"You didn't look so fine this morning. I peeked outside when I got up, and you were sitting on a yard chair, looking forlorn with your Bible in your lap. You hardly said anything at breakfast either."

"I'm okay. I had a long talk with the Lord."

Franny nodded thoughtfully. "Does that mean you did all the talking or He did?"

"For once, I just listened." Kate smiled. "Franny, I've decided this is my last rodeo."

"I was afraid you were going to say that. But I understand."

"Do you?" Kate cocked her head. Was she the only one late to the party?

"Well, sure. You've got everything back in Rebel, including a fella."

A sigh slipped out at the mention of Jess McNally. If only... She'd never have Jess. Too much time and too much distrust stood between them.

"You're not going anywhere yet, are you?" Franny asked.

"No. I'll head out in the morning." She looked at her friend. "Where will you be off to next?"

"To tell you the truth, I've been thinking about going home."

"What?"

"My run was awful on Monday. I'm starting to think it might be time to retire while I can still save face."

"It wasn't awful—"

Franny held up a hand and laughed. "Only a true friend would say that. I'll see how things go, but I've had a look at the competition. I'm not taking home any prize money today." She laughed again. "Good thing I'm not here for the riches."

"Only the fame, right?" Kate returned with a smile.

"Right." Franny smiled right back. "I'll see you back at the trailer, then?"

"Yes."

Kate settled in her seat and couldn't resist a glance at her phone, wondering what Jess was doing today. It was Friday, so maybe he was taking his mom to dialysis, or perhaps he and Willard were checking fence lines. She missed the proud, stubborn cowboy, and that surprised her.

For years, she'd traveled from small towns to big cities, all over the states, to places she didn't even know existed. How far her world had grown from the days when she'd lived in an ancient trailer outside Rebel. Every few months, she'd stop back in Oklahoma to visit her family. Besides her brothers, there wasn't anyone she'd ever missed. She'd schooled her heart not to be sentimental.

Yet here she was thinking about a tall, dark-haired cowboy with laughing gray eyes and a smile that set off a yearning in her heart. She'd always been a solo act, but when she thought about Jess, the idea of a partnership with a man who understood and cared about her seemed irresistible. And also way out of reach.

Her thoughts were interrupted when music began to play over the loudspeakers and the arena noise increased as the bleachers filled. The announcer's booming voice offered the afternoon's highlights. A few timed events followed by roughstock, and that meant bull riding.

Beau Connor was back in the saddle, which would be particularly nostalgic as she hadn't seen the cowboy since Tucson.

Kate glanced at her program in anticipation. Franny was right. She'd be racing against the reigning favorite, Shelby Locker. The woman had won the National Finals Rodeo too many years in a row to remember. Kate was well aware that if she were as good as Locker, she'd still be competing.

The announcer tapped the microphone and cleared his throat. "I understand we have a special guest in the audience tonight. Folks, a few months ago, one of our very own community, bullfighter Kate Rainbolt, did a remarkably heroic thing in the arena up in Tucson in February. Up against Despiadado, one of the meanest bulls to ever hit the chute, her quick actions saved the life of rider Beau Connor. Cowgirl Kate Rainbolt, stand up and make your way down to the arena floor."

Kate's head jerked up, and she sat frozen in her seat, stunned by the announcer's words.

"He's talking to you, Kate. Stand up."

"What?" She whirled around to find Jess in the bleacher aisle, tall and handsome as ever, and he cocked his head toward the arena floor.

"Jess, what are you doing here?"

"Doesn't matter. Head on down there."

She nodded numbly and stood, weak-kneed as the applause, hoots and hollers continued to rise. Jess took her arm and helped her down the steps to the fence, where he gave her a boost over and into the arena.

In the center of the floor, Beau Connor and one of the rodeo officials met her with a microphone in hand. "Ms. Rainbolt, your friends have gotten together to give you a thank-you check to assist with your medical bills. We understand you spent quite a while in the hospital recuperating, due to your brave action."

Everything became a blur as she said thank you into the mic and shook the hands of both men. When a wave of applause rose, Kate looked up into the bleachers. Her gaze scanned the audience. Then it hit her. This was no doubt her last time on the arena floor. The very last time to stand in this particular spot, looking up at the loving faces of the rodeo fans.

Choked up with emotion, she said a silent

goodbye to the life she'd known for the last ten years and sent up a prayer of gratitude for the opportunity.

As the applause died down, she found herself at the gate, squirming as her picture was taken and a reporter for a local paper asked questions for the next edition. When the reporter turned to Beau, Kate slipped away and searched through the crowd for Jess.

It was Franny she found first. The older woman pulled Kate into a warm embrace. "Oh, honey, I'm so proud of you."

"Did you have something to do with this?" Kate asked.

"Of course. I couldn't let what you did go unsung. You could have been killed. Beau, as well."

"What about Jess? What's he doing here?"

"I have no idea. But I can tell you one thing for sure, the man isn't here for the popcorn." Franny nodded to an area near the concession stand where Jess stood silently watching and waiting, as though he had all the time in the world. "I ran into him in the pen area, looking for you."

Kate's heart stuttered when he turned and offered a slow smile. It had been only a week, yet she'd missed him. Missed sparring with him, working with him, and mostly, she'd missed the silent moments between them when words weren't necessary.

"You better go get him before someone else does," Franny said with a chuckle. "I'll be at the trailer if you need me. If I don't see you, I'll trust you came to your senses."

"What?" Kate turned back to Franny.

"Sweetie, your days of looking for something you'll never find are over. That man over there is in love with you. Get a move on."

Get a move on? Could it be that simple? Kate hurried down the walkway toward her future.

Jess leaned against the fence, enjoying the attention Kate was receiving in the walkway. She was a hero, and she'd certainly earned the accolades and this time in the limelight. He was so very proud of her.

Kate spotted him, and her eyes lit up. She

spoke to Franny for a few moments and then crossed the walkway toward him. Was she discussing the job Franny had offered?

Nope. He wouldn't think about that right now. Somehow, some way, he'd find a way to make things between them work. Because he loved her, and he missed her.

Yeah, it had been only a week, and he'd missed so many things. Her stubborn opinions. There was no one who was as much fun to spar with as Kate. Her laughter. He'd missed her laugh and the joy she brought to everything.

When she stood in front of him, he pushed off from the fence and gave her a quick hug. "Congratulations," he said with feigned nonchalance. "You looked good down there."

"Oh, that." She pinked and ducked her head. "That was...unexpected."

"In a good way, right?" he asked.

"Yes. In a good way." She smiled and looked at him hesitantly. "Can we get out of here?"

"Sure. There's a taco drive-through right around the corner."

"Now you're talking my language."

Awkward small talk about the weather replaced real conversation on their way to the truck, and then they were silent. After a few minutes, Kate turned to him. "You never said why you're here."

"Insomnia," Jess said. He signaled and pulled into the fast-food drive-through. A cheerful voice asked for their order, and Kate leaned closer to Jess to see the menu. Close enough that he could feel the warmth of her arm and smell her shampoo. He'd missed that scent.

Mangos.

"Um, sorry," she said when her head brushed his chin.

"No problem."

"I'll take a Number Four and a Number Five with a side of chips and guac. Oh, and a large Dr. Pepper," she said.

Jess laughed and placed his order with hers.

"What's so funny?" she asked.

"I like how you do everything with gusto. I've missed that."

Kate shrugged. "That's a polite way to say I eat like a lumberjack, right?"

"Not at all." He smiled. "Kate, you're a what-you-see-is-what-you-get gal. Unfortunately, I forgot that. I won't again."

She frowned at his admission while he drove up to the next window. When she reached for her wallet, Jess glared at her.

"I've got it," he said. "Haven't we discussed this before?"

"We have, but I wasn't sure if the rules were the same. That was a long time ago."

"Yeah," he said with a nod. "Spring. Here it is early summer."

Summer. It did seem like a lifetime ago that they'd begun this journey. He'd walked into Eagle Donuts in Rebel, Oklahoma, and caught his breath for the second time in his life. That day had changed everything.

They picked up their orders at the second window, and Jess found a shady spot beneath a tree to park the truck. He lowered the windows and released his seat belt.

"So tell me about this insomnia." Kate

pulled her burrito from the paper bag and eyed the thick wrap before digging in.

"First, you tell me what you've been doing," he said. "Made any decisions?"

She nodded and finished her bite, then put a straw into her Dr. Pepper and looked at him. "I'm trying to read the road signs."

"What? That sounds like a Willard-ism."

"It is," she said.

Jess took a bite of his own burrito without tasting anything and then set it down on a napkin on the dash. He'd come here for a reason, and it wasn't to eat.

"Are you going to keep looking for your father?" he asked.

Kate raised a brow as though surprised by his directness. "No, my search for TJ has ended. My brothers helped me with that."

Jess gave a slow shake of his head, all the while thinking and unsure how to proceed. Echoing over and over in his head was the constant realization that he had one chance to get this right. His last chance.

"Now, will you tell me about this insomnia?" Kate asked.

"I haven't had a good night's sleep in days, and I've been praying about what to do. Then it hit me. I've got to change the ending to this story."

"The ending?"

"Yeah. I was wallowing in self-pity when you left, thinking I was a failure again. I couldn't be what my dad wanted, and I couldn't be what you want or need."

"No, Jess, that's not it." Concern filled her eyes.

"Wait. Hear me out."

When she nodded, he continued. "My mother helped me realize that my father's issues were his issues. Not mine. As for us. Ten years ago, you had a quest in your heart that superseded your feelings for me. I should have understood that it wasn't about me. But I didn't."

He swallowed, determined to get the words out. "I've done a lot of thinking since you left. I was wrong, and I'm sorry." He rubbed a hand over his face. "The Lord has given me another opportunity to get things right. I'm not going to blow it this time. I'm here to fight for us. If you want to be on the circuit, working for Franny or whatever, then I'll support that."

"You will?"

"Yeah. I'm no different than my father if I presume to tell you what you should do with your future. If you want to rodeo, we'll find a way to make it work. Just give what I think we have a chance."

Jess gathered courage when her eyes met his. There was something in the blue depths that said she cared. He'd bank on that for now.

She wiped her lips with a napkin and cocked her head. "Jess, I think we can agree that I'm at least as prideful as you are. You're the best thing that ever happened to me, and I pushed you away. I guess the truth is I've spent my entire life pushing away most of the people who tried to get close, certain they'd leave me. After all, the one man who should have loved me more than anything did."

At the admission, Kate swallowed hard and blinked, her eyes moist, and his heart ached for her.

"Jess, I've spent a lot of time trying to fix the past. I was so certain I would find him. I was sure that if I did and he knew how much I loved him, my father would come home."

"Remember what you told Olive?" Jess asked. "Your worth is unchanged in the sight of the Lord. It's unchanged in my eyes too, Kate. I'm bursting with pride at the woman you are."

"Thank you," she murmured. "I have a lot of people who care about me, and I haven't spent nearly enough time telling them how much I care, including you." She paused. "Please forgive me, Jess."

"Nothing to forgive. We both had a lot of mud to slog through to get to where we are. I'm thinking it's time we both give as much time to our future as we have given to our past."

"I agree. I'm ready to look to the future."

"Yeah?" His heart slammed against his chest as he prayed that for once they were riding horses in the same direction. "Kate, I want a future with you. Wherever that may be."

She sighed. "Finally, we agree on something."

"We do?"

"Yes. I love you, Jess."

For a moment, he stared out the window, both shocked and savoring the words he hadn't expected to hear.

"Aren't you going to say something?" Kate asked.

"Yeah, I am." He took the burrito and the Dr. Pepper from her hands and placed them on the dash. "I love you too, Kate. Probably never stopped loving you."

"Oh, Jess," she breathed.

He played with the purple tips of her hair, twirling them around his fingers. "Mind if I seal the deal?"

She sighed. "I thought you'd never ask."

He cupped her cheek with his hand and looked down at the face he'd loved for so long. "I love you," he whispered before his lips touched hers.

Epilogue

"But, Jess, I don't want a fancy church wedding." Kate smiled with excitement as the truck passed the Rebel city-limits sign. Soon, she'd be home. It was four days post–laparoscopic surgery to donate a kidney, and she was ready for her little house, her cat and a future with her husband.

A warm September morning breeze streamed through the open truck windows, and the sweet, welcoming scent of recently mowed grass welcomed her. The redbud leaves had turned a canary yellow and seemed to be guiding her home.

When the sunlight bounced off the rings on Kate's finger, she held up her hand to admire the wedding band and engagement ring. A sweetheart diamond had been set in the middle of two smaller side stones. They represented his, hers and theirs. Two hearts united.

Mrs. Jess McNally. She was blessed beyond measure.

"I love this ring," she murmured.

Jess took his hand off the steering wheel for a moment to squeeze her fingers gently. Love and the promise of tomorrow shone in his eyes.

"Just think about it, Kate. I don't want you to regret that we got married by a justice of the peace in St. Francis Hospital and that you wore a hospital gown and I wore my Levis."

"No one ever had a wedding like ours, Jess. It was a spontaneous expression of love. Besides, we had cake. Daisy brought us that beautiful lemon-filled cake, and our family was present. Even your mother. What else could we want?"

"Surely you want a church wedding, something you can look back on."

"No. That's not what I want at all."

"Kate, Pastor Tuttle was still in his golf shorts."

She gave an adamant shake of her head. "The Lord was in that hospital room, and that's good enough for me." It was the wedding she'd never dreamed of, and everything she wanted. No fancy gazebo ceremony could even compare. It was a wedding she'd tell her children about.

"Look at that picket fence," Jess murmured as he pulled the truck into the drive of the little house that would now be theirs. "It's pretty sad. Shall we get rid of it?"

"A new coat of paint should fix it, right? Someday we might have kids in that yard, and we'll want them safe."

Jess jerked his head around to meet her gaze. "What did you say?"

"I said someday. The doctor said at least six months post-op."

He opened and closed his mouth before finally speaking. "Every time I've mentioned children, you've changed the subject."

"That's because I was afraid. I'm not now." Kate smiled. No, there was nothing to fear about her future anymore.

"Now that I've mastered the slow cooker," she continued. "I'm confident that cereal won't be the only thing I can dish up." She unfastened her seat belt and leaned close to press a quick kiss to his lips. "And everything will be served with a side of love. Plenty of love."

Jess chuckled. "We have lots of that to go around."

For a long moment, Kate simply stared at the handsome face of the cowboy she loved so very much. "I love you, Jess McNally."

"I love you, Katherine Margaret Rainbolt McNally."

Kate grinned. "Come on. Let's get inside." She pushed open her door.

"Hey, hey, wait. I'll help you down."

"Stop fussing. I'm fine."

"That's what you always say." Despite her protests, he carefully eased her to the pavement.

"Well, it's true. I'm fine. They wouldn't have discharged me if I wasn't okay." She looked around. "I want to see Einstein soon too."

"Kate, you just had major surgery."

"Never felt better." She paused. "When did you last check in with your mom?"

"Right before we left the hospital. They'll discharge her tomorrow. She's still insisting on staying in her own house and refusing to be admitted to the rehab center in Tulsa."

"I love that woman." Kate laughed. "She warned us she was going to insist."

"She's as stubborn as you are," Jess said.

"Yes. Her best feature." She smiled. "You called the nursing agency Tucker recommended?"

"Yep. Nurses are set up for as long as the doctor advises."

Kate reached for her tote bag and grimaced as her incisions pulled.

"I've got your bag." He met her gaze. "You don't have to be tough. It's okay to ask for help."

"I'm learning." Yes, she was learning that Jess would always be there for her. She wrapped an arm around his, and they started up the walk to the house. She stopped at the sight of two large glazed clay pots filled with autumn flowers. Deep burgundy and golden chrysanthemums and tall purple fountain grass.

"Who did this?" Kate asked. "So pretty."

"Those are courtesy of your sisters-in law. Nicole made the pots, and Claire and Daisy filled them."

When she stepped over the threshold, she realized her house was filled with people. They must have walked over from the admin building to surprise her.

It was a welcome surprise to see the faces of everyone she loved. Mitch and Daisy and their crew were present. Reece and Claire and their kids. Tucker and Jena and the twins, along with Jena's daughter, Dee, visiting from college. Nicole was present with Finn Hardy. She spied Willard Cornell swiping one of Daisy's muffins from the buffet table. He looked up and winked.

Even Violet and Chef Luna were in attendance.

Kate's heart swelled with the realization that she was so well loved.

As the chatter of welcomes continued, Olive wiggled through the group of adults and children until she was in front of Kate. She was holding Bella in her arms. "Aunt Kate, I'm so glad you're home. Bella and I missed you."

"I missed you both too." Kate looked up, her gaze touching each person in the room and finally landing on Jess. Her heart ached with thanksgiving. Everything she needed was right here in this room and in this town.

The past had brought her here, and it was time to start living the life the Lord had put in front of her. Yes, it was time. Time to put down roots and call Rebel Ranch home.

* * * * *

*If you enjoyed this emotional romance
from Tina Radcliffe,
don't miss the other
Hearts of Oklahoma stories:*

Finding the Road Home
Ready to Trust
His Holiday Prayer

Available now from Love Inspired.

*Find more great reads at
www.LoveInspired.com.*

Dear Reader,

Thank you so much for journeying with me to Rebel, Oklahoma, to meet the Rainbolt clan. I have fallen in love with Mitch, Reece, Tucker and Kate and hope that you have too.

As the only female in the family, Kate was a treat to write. Her character was inspired by Shakespeare's Kate in *The Taming of the Shrew*. Kate Rainbolt evolves, and she realizes that stepping away from the independence of her rodeo life into the seemingly dependent role as a partner in a ranch and eventually in a marriage is merely a new opportunity to express herself. She also realizes that Jess McNally loves her not in spite of who she is but because of who she is.

Jess and Kate's romance is a two-step dance. One step forward and two steps back as they discover God's ever-present and unconditional love and find their happily-ever-after.

Do drop me a note and let me know what your favorite parts of this story were. I can be reached through my website, www.tina-radcliffe.com, where you can also find Kate's slow-cooker recipes, which have been taste tested by me.

Enjoy!

Sincerely,
Tina Radcliffe